HELL'S KITCHEN

ALSO BY BENJAMIN APPEL

DOCUMENTARY
The People Talk
With Many Voices

NOVELS
Brain Guy
The Powerhouse
Fortress in the Rice
Life and Death of a Tough Guy
The Funhouse
A Time of Fortune
The Devil and W. Kaspar

FOR YOUNG READERS
The Klondike Gold Rush
Age of Dictators
Man and Magic
The Fantastic Mirror

BENJAMIN APPEL

HELL'S KITCHEN

PANTHEON BOOKS

Library of Congress Cataloging in Publication Data

Appel, Benjamin, 1907– Hell's Kitchen.
SUMMARY: Relates the experiences of four boys growing up
in New York City's Hell's Kitchen during the period
of the first World War.
1. Friendship—Fiction.   2. New York (City)—Fiction.
3. City and town life—Fiction.   I. Title.
PZ7.A640n   [Fic.]   76–44014   ISBN 0–394–83236–1
0 9 8 7 6 5 4 3 2 1

For the kids I used to play with in Hell's Kitchen

Frankie Da Vita
Marcel During
Ramon Fernandez
Nicholas Kotchkaves
Izzy Mann
Georgie Moore
Frankie Silver
Jakey Teicher
    and for
Silvana

HELL'S KITCHEN

PART ONE

THE 1-4-ALLS

"We'll be wun for all
'gainst the Irish micks. . . ."

ONE

"Suppose the micks over Thirty-sevent' was the first to call themself the 1-4-Alls? They don't own that name! We can call ourself any damn thing we want!"

Dutch's voice, the changing voice of a thirteen-year-old, girlish one second and man-husky the next, shrilled loud and clear in the darkening backyard where they had been playing baseball, two-a-side, Dutch and Paulie vs. Georgie and Angie, the score 47 to 29 in the thirty-first inning; the game was called when the baseball seemed to melt away like a scoop of vanilla ice cream. Between the two enclosing fences the backyard was a bluish square, the row of sheds at the far end a dusky rose, the four shadowy figures strangely alike, their faces white and spooky and raceless.

Was Dutch Yaeger a smelly sauerkraut, Paulie Bolkonski a dumb polack, Georgie Alston a lousy limey, Angie a garlic-eating wop? That they were to the Irish kids who lived on their block and all the other blocks in the old Hell's Kitchen district over on the West Side of Manhattan. If you weren't a true son of Erin born your name was mud. And such being the case, you deserved what you got: a free set of knuckles or a kick in the slats.

"1-4-All's perfeck!" Dutch argued.

"Yuh bet!" Angie said.

"Stink on it!" Paulie yelled. "Me, I'm no mick copycat!"

"Lissen a minute an' tell me this, Paulie," Dutch demanded. "Ain't there four o' us? Right? That's why it's perfeck."

"Perfect, my ass!" Georgie hollered. He was fourteen, older than the others by a year, and in his opinion smarter than all three put together.

For over a week Dutch, like a dog retrieving a stick, had been bringing up what he called the *perfect* name for their club, with Georgie and Paulie just as stubbornly throwing it back at him.

"Perfeck!" Dutch screamed. "Why cancha get that into your dumb noodle?"

"Yeah!" Angie agreed.

"Yeh yeh yeh!" Georgie mimicked. "Angie the yeh guy!"

For a few minutes it seemed as if every boy on the block —Thirty-eighth Street between Eighth and Ninth avenues —had piled into that backyard in a contest to see who could holler the loudest.

When the shouting match ended, Paulie asked, "Why can't we be Indyuns like we usta?"

Dutch let loose with a mocking war whoop. "Grow up, Paulie!"

Paulie cursed, and puckering up his lips, he aimed at a crayoned heart drawn on one of the shed doors, a black blob in the dark, before shooting out a mouthful of spit. The "oyster," as they called it, hit an inch off target.

"I'll show yuh!" Angie challenged him. "A bull's-eye!"

he yelled triumphantly after spitting his oyster.

"Bullshit, hoss-shit, pigeonshit pie!" Paulie chanted as Dutch, a self-appointed referee, declared Angie the winner —and since he and Angie were for the name 1-4-All, that settled it.

"We ain't micks—" Paulie began.

"Goddammit, Paulie, I hate the micks as much as you," Dutch pleaded with him. "Looka, Paulie, we'd be one for all *against* the micks!"

That argument won Georgie over. And when Dutch asked Paulie if he wanted to be a spoilsport, the grumbling boy gave in. Angie shouted hooray; Georgie tossed his mitt up on the air, caught it, and said he didn't know about the rest of them, but he was going home to eat supper. They all headed toward the rear door of the tenement, their black cotton stockings dyed even blacker in the descending dark. All of them wore black cotton stockings, knee pants, and floppy caps; it was a uniform almost in the year 1917. A fellow only put on long pants—"longies"—when he graduated from public school.

Dutch peered at a cat slinking along the top of one of the fences. "Scat!" he yelled, as if the creeping shadow with the flashing green eyes were the enemy.

Solid Irish that neighborhood, block after block of four- and five-story tenements with black iron fire escapes, the gutters cobblestoned, the sidewalks slate blue with here and there the worn red brick laid down in Civil War times. Five avenues wide and each avenue numbered: Eighth Avenue had its moving-picture houses—Ye Olde Drury Lane on the corner of Forty-second, the Arena, and the Gem; a piano player up front under the silent screen, and as he played an usher paraded the aisles spraying perfume out of his squirt gun to tone down the smells of the sleeping bums; Ninth Avenue always a-roar with the elevated trains, the trollies underneath the tracks jangling past the stores; and every Saturday the horse-and-wagon fruit and vegetable peddlers lining the curbs, the sidewalks a sardine crush of housewives come to shop in Paddy's Market; Tenth and Eleventh and Twelfth avenues, and beyond Twelfth—the widest avenue of them all—the great Hudson flowing to the sea, carpeted in pure blue or cloudy green or sunset gold.

A little Dublin, the Tammany politicians said when they were talking fancy. But it was Hell's Kitchen to everybody else: the cops who walked their beats in pairs, ever on the lookout for a flying rooftop brick; the mothers weeping for sons cooling their heels in the Tombs or up the river in Sing Sing; the saloonkeepers who kept sawed-off baseball bats or some other pacifier handy for the Saturday-night dock wallopers or teamsters who, with a shot of whiskey too many and tired maybe of debating whether America should've gone to war against Kaiser Bill or stayed the hell out, were always ready to wreck the joint. Hell's Kitchen it was to the teachers in Public School 32 where any kid labeled a "teacher's pet" or a "bookworm" would have his dumb head knocked off—knocked off twice for good measure if he was a dutchie, polack, limey, wop, jewboy, frenchy, spick, greaseball, or greeky.

As they left the backyard, Dutch Yaeger, Paulie Bolkonski, Georgie Alston, and Angie Cuomo never imagined that in a few years the 1-4-Alls (*No Micks Allowed,* their slogan) would be another Hell's Kitchen legend.

Not even Paulie had the imagination to foresee the future. Paulie, who every night in the janitor's flat behind the stairs where he lived with his widowed mother and two little sisters, slipped through the pages of a library book into times long gone when the Indian tribes roamed an America without cities. . . .

The very next day they began to clean up the backyard shed that belonged to Dutch's family. With brooms borrowed from Paulie's mother, the janitor of the house —355 West 38th—where Dutch's family lived on the third floor and Paulie's in the flat behind the stairs, they swept up the dust and the spider webs, mopped the jagged pieces of slate that some forgotten tenant had set down on the packed earth floor.

"Gonna be the best club inna whole world," Dutch gloated as they carried in a half dozen fruit boxes to serve as chairs and table.

Saturday, at nine o'clock, as they had agreed the day before, they met outside the tenement. Thirty-eighth Street was also the home block for Georgie, whose parents had a flat up near Eighth; and for Angie, whose father sat all day in his shoe repair shop down near Ninth, hammering heels and cutting leather soles, two caged canaries keeping him company.

That July morning the sunlit backyard shone like a brand new penny. Happy and excited, they sidestepped the rain dripping from clotheslines strung across the yard and hung with freshly washed laundry; the narrow door of the cleaned-up shed seemed to widen and lengthen as they neared it, the peeling red paint spanking bright in their eyes. They crowded inside, and Dutch shut the door behind them.

"1-4-All, that's us!" he exclaimed, and reaching up to a shelf, he took down a bottle with a half-burned candle stuck in its neck. He lit the candle and placed the bottle on the fruit-box table. "Jeez!" he murmured rapturously, only to frown a second later at a ray of sunlight pouring in through a knothole in the closed door. "Hey, Angie, plug that damn hole!" he yelled.

"With what?" Angie asked.

Georgie grinned. "With your sister Mary's drawers."

"Bastid, doncha talk that way 'bout my sister!"

Paulie flushed. These last few months he could never see Angie's sister without feeling funny, his heart doing a hop, skip, jump, his tongue freezing in his mouth. A funny feeling, a secret feeling that he kept to himself.

"Angie's right," he heard himself saying as if he were far away, not in the candlelit shed but floating somewhere, and next to him a girl who could only have been Mary— black her eyes, black her hair, and dressed in a long gown as golden as the light shining through the door.

Dutch rammed a handkerchief into the knothole. The soft glow of the candle gilded the faces of the boys. In the shed's half-shadow Dutch and Paulie might have been twins. They were the same age, thirteen going on fourteen, both of them big and blond, their hair as yellow as the corn that would be sold come August in Paddy's

Market under the El. Light blue their eyes, but only a nearsighted person—"a cockeye"—would've mixed them up. Dutch's face was round as a melon, his nose shaped like a wedge. "It's a reg'lar pig snout!" the Irish kids at P.S. 32 had said many a time, pointing at his wide nostrils. "Yuh kin drop a coupla pennies in!" As to Paulie the Irish had agreed long ago, with indisputable authority of sheer numbers, that all polacks, even nice-looking ones like Paulie, had faces like horses.

Angie, to the Irish kids, was just another "wop, a ginzo . . . spaghetti." Georgie "a lousy limey—black Prottystant." Georgie's dark brown hair, soft and sleek as glove leather, and his unusually large dark eyes under finely shaped brows, might get an Irish girl oohing and ahing—but not her brothers. They had it in for Georgie, not only because of his religion or his handsome face, but for the way he spoke. "Bastid comes from Massa-choosetts, from some hick town called Woods Hole Ass Hole."

Safe in their candlelit shed, like four mice with no cats to worry about, they smiled when Dutch rapped on the box table and announced that this was the first meeting of the Thirty-eighth Street 1-4-Alls.

"Hooray!" said Angie.

"Three cheers for the red, white, and blue," said Georgie.

"What about the boat?" Paulie asked.

Dutch nodded and reached up to a shelf and took down the boat.

The boat was what made them special. Paulie had carved it out of a block of pine wood, painting the hull and three masts with black stove polish; the sails and flag scissored out

11

of a couple of white handkerchiefs Georgie'd stolen at R. H. Macy's department store on Thirty-fourth Street. All smiles now, Paulie proudly lifted the drooping flag on which he'd drawn a skull and crossbones, the club's motto —*1-4-All*—lettered underneath it.

"The foist thing today is who's gonna be the leader?" Dutch asked.

"Yuh!" Angie said, and Georgie, winking at Paulie, seconded the motion.

With that settled, they all began talking of what to do that day? Angie was for riding the Weehawken Ferry over to New Jersey. They could hike up the Palisades or swim in the river.

"What about the ol' fort in Central Park?" Paulie suggested. "Maybe the door'll be open this time an' we'll find a musket or a powder horn—"

"Find shit!" Georgie said, shaking his head with exaggerated pity. "Paulie, Dutch's right about you. You'll never grow up!"

"Stink on yuh, Georgie!" Paulie shouted. "It's a real fort."

And that it was. When he had told Miss Yates, his seventh-grade teacher, about the fort she had spoken about the Revolutionary War. Back then the fort had been a lookout for Washington's fighting men.

"Sure it's real," Georgie said, "but if you think there's any old muskets laying around, you're cuckoo."

"Coo-koo!" Dutch laughed.

"Coo-koo!" Angie echoed.

Then Georgie said Central Park wasn't a bad idea. They

could go to the zoo, swipe some peanuts from the peanut man, feed the elephants and make the monkeys spit.

Paulie wasn't listening. Although his knees rubbed against Angie's, he had sailed off on the pirate ship he'd carved. He only stirred when Dutch shouted: "Le's get goin'!"

All four rushed out of the shed.

TWO

PAULIE stirred as his mother's voice reached him from
the far end of the long black tunnel that separated
night from day. He yawned, groping for the ten-pound
dumbbell on the chair alongside his white enameled cot.
He picked it up with his right hand, raised it over his head,
lowered it, all the while counting silently: one, two, three,
four. . . . When his lips shaped the number *twenty* he
switched to his left hand. The ceiling floating above had
steadied; he was wide awake now. The exercises had
cleared his head.

Somewhere it was bright early morning, if not in his hall
bedroom. The single window on the air shaft was untouched by the sun shining on the roof five stories above.
It was just as dark in the room where his two sisters slept.
Only the kitchen, fronting on the backyard, was light, even
on rainy days.

Again his mother called. "The chickens must be fed, the
cows milked," she said in Polish, the language of home.

"I'm up!" he answered in the language of the street.
Chickens! Cows! That was his mother, always joking, as if
she were as strong as she used to be.

From underneath the cot he retrieved his long cotton stockings. Next, the pants. He put them on over the underwear that he wore all week, night and day, like a second skin. Fully dressed at last, his shoes buttoned, he stood up and began to shadowbox.

He shot out his trusty left and floored the enemies of class and street. There lay the outstretched body of Jimmy Hanley! A right to the jaw took care of Spider O'Toole! Somewhere a fight crowd cheered, somewhere the fans shouted: *Look at Paulie! The Champ! The Polish Tiger!*

When he stepped into the kitchen his mother greeted him. "*Dzien dobry*—good morning."

"*Dobry*," he replied.

Through the white-curtained windows the early-morning light flooded the kitchen. Light splintered the shining nickel trim of the black coal stove, polished the knees of the Christ on the wall crucifix.

His mother stooped as he went forward to kiss her. For a second she held him tight, then she straightened. She was a big woman, but the bigness, as he knew, wasn't real. Her cheeks had caved in under her high cheekbones, her lips, once as red as those of his little sisters Ava and Christina, had become colorless. Only the long brown hair fastened in a bun at the back of her head hadn't changed. As he washed at the sink she asked him if he was hungry. "Or is that a foolish question to ask a boy growing like a birch?"

At the gas range alongside the sink his mother was frying some leftover cold potatoes. She stirred them with a fork, cracked open an egg. He licked his lips as the egg sizzled in the pan.

"A growing boy should have two eggs or even three," she said. "And you work like a man—"

"Wun's enuf, mama." He seldom answered her in Polish. Polish was for the greenhorns off the boat.

Her shoulders sagged when she sat down at the table. Deep inside him something trembled and quivered.

"Mama, do you feel sick?" he asked.

"No," she said and gazed at him with eyes as blue as his own; an intense look gone in a second. He had a feeling he had seen a stranger.

She guessed what was in his mind and with a rueful smile reminded him that she was no longer young.

After breakfast he filled a pail with hot water, and clutching a broom and two mops in his free hand, he climbed to the top floor. There wasn't a sound behind the doors of the flats; the men off to work on the docks or in the factories and warehouses, the women either asleep or getting ready to go shopping. He lowered the pail and swept the long hallway clean of cigarette stubs, scraps of paper, and the dirt brought into the house by rain-wet shoes. This done, he dipped a mop into the pail and swished it along the floor boards, the strands of the mop curling out like a bunch of skinny wet worms. Sweat shone on his forehead. He blew off the beads trickling down to the end of his nose, and with the dry mop he sponged up the watery patches. Two floors today and the rest tomorrow, he thought.

When he met Dutch and Georgie and Angie in their clubhouse shed he sang out an old Hell's Kitchen jingle: "Wun, two, t'ree a-leary, who's drinkin' beer with Missus Leary . . ."

Dutch shook his head and said the guy was drunk. Crazy, said Georgie. Angie said nothing, grinning.

"I'm not drunk an' I'm not crazy!" Paulie shouted happily. "I'm just through workin', yuh guys!"

Where did the summer days go, the blue-sky mornings on the Weehawken Ferry over to New Jersey and the Palisade walls of gray stone, the swims in the river, Dutch yelling: "Last wun in stinks on ice!" The rainy days when they sat smoking in the candlelit shed, maybe slicing up a watermelon swiped from Paddy's Market, the pirate ship with its 1-4-All flag sailing in golden light on a golden sea. There were days when Angie had to work for his old man, and passing the shoe repair shop, they would wave at the poor guy polishing shoes, hammering heels or cutting leather into the shape of footprints. There were days when Paulie stayed behind, sweeping and mopping every single one of the five floors of the house. And there was the Saturday in August when he painted the door of their flat a brilliant yellow to please his mother.

"In the village where I was born," she had said, "summer was the yellow month. The sun was yellow, the flowers were yellow, the wheat was yellow. Yellow was the color of my youth and one day I painted the door of our home yellow."

Go try and explain that to a dumb ox like Dutch.

"So your ol' lady wanted a yeller door," Dutch'd said.

"Yeh," Paulie'd answered, "what's wrong wit' that?"

"Nothin', but what for?"

"She's from Po-land where there was yeller flowers an' the yeller stuff growin' what they make bread out of."

"So that's why? But didn' yuh haffta pay for that yeller paint?"

"How many times must I tell yuh we hadda pay . . ."

Where had the summer gone, the baseball games in the backyard or out in the gutter, Georgie in a brand new baseball cap saying, "If you guys were game you could swipe your own at Macy's or one of them other big stores!" and all of them staring at Georgie, not because he'd done something great but because he made it sound great. There were the still evenings, the stars high above the clotheslines in the backyard, white-pointed diamonds strung across the sky, the four of them behind the closed door of the 1-4-All shed, Paulie silent when they talked about girls, Georgie the big noise bragging how he'd taken Alice Halloran up to the roof—Dirty Alice as every sniggering kid on the block called her—and if it wasn't Alice some other girl.

Go believe Georgie! Listen to him and you'd think his old man was the captain on the Weehawken Ferry when all he was was a deckhand, no better than Angie's father the shoemaker or Dutch's who was a pigsticker in the slaughter-house on Eleventh.

"My ol' man drove a beer wagon," Paulie would say, his lips sewed tight when they tried to pump him on how his old man got himself killed. He would either clam up or else sing out the song every Hell's Kitchen kid knew by heart: "My ol' man number one, he plays nik nak onna drum, nik nak pollywog gingasaw, my ol' man can play no more. . . . My ol' man number two, he plays nik nak onna shoe—"

"Never mind that shit!" they would yell, Dutch hollering the loudest. "Betcha your ol' man got hisself killed by some drunky mick."

The summer had gone, but fear remained like an ice-hard snowman no season could thaw. It appeared out of nowhere and where least expected—out of a hallway on the library block, Fortieth Street between Ninth and Tenth, cursing the bookworms, ripping the pages of their library books and throwing them into the gutter.

"What the hell d'yuh haffta go to the liberry?" was Dutch's sole comment when Paulie told how he'd been caught. Dutch read the funnies *Krazy Kat* and the *Katzenjammer Kids*—they had a stupid old library book beat a mile.

"Go or not go," Georgie'd said, "The micks'll get you anyway."

Get you on the street, get you under the El over at Paddy's Market, get you on the summer docks, get you on Halloween. Never sleeping, waiting behind the walls of a street-corner snow fort, and winter or summer, always ready with a fist for any bastard who wasn't a true son of Erin.

Safe and secure in their candlelit shed, they cursed the micks. And when they crossed the backyard, the hour late, homeward bound, Dutch maybe, or Georgie, or Paulie, or even little Angie—who was so peaceful by nature that they thought of him as the mouse of the bunch—would swear that someday he was going to get even with the micks.

Someday in a summer still to come . . .

THREE

Sの EPTEMBER blew in bright as the flags flapping on Ninth Avenue. It was a patriotic year, the store windows a carnival of war posters. There was President Wilson inviting everyone to read the slogan he had given the nation: *The War to Save Democracy*. And Uncle Sam in a star-spangled high hat and white chin whiskers brandishing a finger at the passersby.

September was school again! Teachers' dirty looks again!

Pushing open the vestibule door of the house where he lived, his kid brother and sister behind him, Dutch peered up at the sky. Blue, radiant, weightless, it flew like a kite above the tin cornices of the red brick tenements on the other side of the street.

The sky said: *Play hookey*.

School was for punks. No place for him when he could do a million zillion things more fun than sitting in Mr. Finley's class with the pictures of the Presidents stuck up on the wall: Old George Washington who'd never told a lie—"Believe that," Mr. Finley's pupils had roared, "an' I'll tell yuh anodder!"—and Old Abe Lincoln who'd freed the slaves and Old Woodrow Wilson who'd declared war on Germany.

Dutch's pale blue eyes shifted to the scrubbed pink-penny faces of his brother, Emil, and sister, Gertrude. They had followed him down the stairs, their mother warning them as she did every school morning to stay close to their big brother, to be careful crossing the streets. Not that Emil and Gertrude couldn't go to school by themselves; they were old enough. Emil was eleven and Gertrude ten, no kindergarten babies. What worried Mrs. Yaeger was the neighborhood—*der Kuche von Teufel*—Hell's Kitchen. A true name, where anything bad could happen.

Gertie, Dutch knew, wouldn't rat on him if he played hookey, but you couldn't trust Emil with a wooden nickel. He'd snitch to the old man, and the old man would pull his belt off his pants and Ouch!

Behind him the vestibule door creaked. "Hey," he greeted Paulie, whose two sisters Ava and Christina, were trailing their big brother.

"Paulie," Dutch said meaningfully, holding up his left hand, the thumb tucked into the palm, the four fingers stiff and upright. It was the secret 1-4-All sign. "Ant-way ay-pay ook-ay?" he jabbered, talking the Chinkee-Chinese of the streets, talking fast so Emil wouldn't catch on.

"Yuh wanna play hookey?" Emil translated instantly and although he was only eleven years old he sounded like the truant officer himself.

"Naw, not me, Emil!" Dutch protested. "I just forgot one o' my books. Yeh, Emil! Hones' to God! So why doncha take Gertie to school—"

"I'll tell papa 'less yuh take me with youse!"

Dutch groaned. "Lousy stool pigeon! Doidy rat!"

"Sticks an' stones kin break my bones, names kin never hoit me," Emil sang.

The three little girls listened without a word, neat and spotless in their white middy blouses and dark skirts, their hair brushed and ribboned. They could have been strays from another world, speaking their own language, remote from the concerns of their big brothers. They liked school, they never played hookey. They were girls.

Dutch was pleading with Emil. He promised—*"Cross my heart hope to die!"*—to take him the next time, but the smaller boy kept parroting, "Now—now—" Dutch cursed and then his expression changed as if he had chewed on a lump of sugar. "Hey, Emil! Looka this!" He fetched a small object out of his pocket. Slowly he opened his fingers on a fly cage hollowed out of a whiskey cork, its single window barred with five or six pins.

"Yuh wanna gimme it?" Emil asked suspiciously. "No tricks? Chickee-choo?"

"Chickee-chee," Dutch said, sealing the bargain.

Emil took the fly cage and shook it. The fly imprisoned behind the glinting silvery pins buzzed. Dutch glanced down at the strapped books he held in one hand and said he'd forgotten his geography book. He asked Paulie to wait for him; Emil'd bring Paulie's sisters and Gertie to school. The three little girls seemed deaf to his alibi, their eyes shut on the little business of the fly cage. When Emil marched them off, they followed like soldiers obeying a corporal.

"Maybe we should-a gone to school?" Paulie muttered.

"What're yuh, a teacher's pet all-a sudden?"

"Take that back or I'll sock yuh one!"

They glared at each other like two mongrels growling over a bone. A bunch of passing dock wallopers bound for the waterfront west of Ninth, wearing their baling hooks in their belts or around their necks like iron collars, urged the two boys to fight it out. Paulie glanced at the men and lowered his right fist. Whispering, he reminded Dutch that they were 1-4-Alls.

Dutch's clenched lips parted, and he shook his shaggy blond head. "An' me the leader. Some leader!"

The disappointed dock wallopers walked on.

"The hell with 'em an' the hell with school!" Dutch grinned.

"Yuh said a mouthful!" Paulie shouted joyfully.

It was a perfect day to go down the docks where the ferryboats churned the green water whiter than the milk ladled out of the metal cans at the Sheffield store on Ninth, or go over to Forty-second Street and Times Square with its tobacco stores guarded by painted wooden Indians and beg the men coming out for the picture cards inside their packs of Helmar or Sweet Caporal cigarettes. Pictures of baseball stars like Ty Cobb or heavyweight champs like John L. Sullivan.

Mr. Finley, having finished calling the roll and marking the "absents" in his attendance book—among them Henry (Dutch) Yaeger and Paul Bolkonski—got up from his desk. Instantly, the class became quiet, the whisperers silent, the spitballers inactive. Mr. Findley had the eye of an eagle, and the strong arm of a bouncer in a saloon.

"Alston!" Mr. Finley said. "Get up!"

Georgie Alston jumped out of his seat. "Yes, sir," he answered with a smile.

No one else in the class had the nerve to smile when Mr. Finley said *Get up!* And now many a boy was thinking, you had to hand it to Black Georgie, limey or no limey.

"Alston, did you see Yaeger or Bolkonski this morning?"

"No, sir."

"You live on the same street," he continued like a gimlet-eyed detective putting one clue alongside another.

"Yes, sir, but I never see them, sir."

A lie, a big fat whopper of a lie. Everybody in the hushed classroom, teacher and students, knew it. From somewhere in the back seats there was a half-suppressed snort of admiration. The whisperers began whispering again, the throat garglers gargled, the feet shufflers scraped the soles of their shoes on the floor.

"Stop!" Mr. Finley commanded. The mouths of the class shut tight like purses whose strings had been pulled. "Alston, come forward!" He pointed at the lithograph of a white-wigged Washington and stated that Washington believed in the truth. "Alston, you will stand in front of his picture until you are ready to admit that you lied—"

"Excuse me, sir, I didn't lie. I mean, I see them on the street, but they're nobody to me—"

"Excuse *me*," the teacher interrupted ironically. "They're nothing but strangers? When you leave class with Yaeger and Bolkonski, or talk with them, you are just being polite?"

The class laughed as Georgie walked up front. He was still smiling, a faint smile. To Mr. Finley it had the edge of a knife. Once again he was oppressed by the feeling that all his years in this school had been a waste. Sooner or later even boys for whom he had some hopes were ground down like blackboard chalk. If Georgie Alston was born for trouble, Paulie Bolkonski had seemed like a boy who might have escaped Hell's Kitchen. Attentive, polite, a good student—and yet here he was following that wild Yaeger boy like a puppy on a leash.

FOUR

THE two hookey players had sneaked back into the house to hide their books.

"Yuh go first," Paulie whispered. Ever since his father's death two years ago the dank cellar with its sagging wooden beams had reminded him of the open grave in the cemetery; the raw earth piled up like some terrible mouth waiting to swallow the coffin; his sisters clutching his mother's black skirt as Father McGinley prayed in Latin, the language spoken by the saints and that his father would speak when he came to heaven.

The cellar stairs creaked as the two boys descended. Paulie peered into the darkness. Dutch struck a match; the tiny yellow flare burst into a golden ball after he lit a candle. The coal bins showed themselves, their locks glittering like metal eyes. Dutch stuck the candle down in its own melt on a wooden horse, groped for the keys in his pocket. He unlocked the bin on which his old man'd painted his name: *Yaeger*. Tossed his books and Paulie's inside, grinned, digging his hand into his pocket and taking out a cardboard cigarette container that had once held Fatimas. He flipped the lid open to a dozen or so half-smoked butts scavenged off the streets.

26

"Le's go," Paulie muttered.

"Nah, gotta wait til the micks're all in school."

Paulie glanced over his shoulder. They were alone and not alone, but he couldn't tell Dutch that he was afraid of ghosts. He had never been afraid of the cellar but after his father's funeral it had become a haunted place, the closed doors of the bins upended coffins with something lurking in the shadows, sharp of teeth like a sewer rat.

"Here," said Dutch, holding out the cigarettes.

"I don't feel like smokin'."

"You're in trainin', huh?" Dutch laughed. "Jeez, wotta pip! Even the champs smoke between fights. Jess Willard the heavyweight champ, alla them! I smoke an' I don't fool around with no dumbbells like yuh!" And clenching his right arm, he said, "Just feel that muscle, Paulie!"

"Le's go—"

"What's the rush?"

"I hate it here."

" 'Cause it's dark?"

" 'Cause it's down."

"Down? Sure it's down. All cellars gotta be down or they wouldn't be cellars. Jeez, Paulie, if yuh ain't the funny one!" And raising his hand he revolved a stiffened fore-finger in front of his temple. Like some pencil it inscribed the cuckoo sign on the thin air. Cuckoo, mad, crazy as a loon.

Paulie burst out. "Your ol' man ain't dead!"

Side by side the two boys walked up Ninth, the letters on the plate-glass windows spelling out a secret message for them alone: *School was for punks!*

They stopped in front of a druggist's to peer at a jar of black leeches.

"They're like snot!" Paulie exclaimed, fascinated. "I'd rather have a black eye than put wunna them t'ings on!"

Arguing about cures for black eyes and bloody noses, they went on. Dutch's nostrils dilated as they neared a delicatessen. Outside the door there was a barrel of sauerkraut painted red, white, and blue, to which a sign was attached: *Liberty Cabbage*.

Dutch sniffed. "Get a whiff o' that!" he said.

"Yuh know why nobody swipes sauerkraut?" Paulie said thoughtfully. "It just come to me."

"Okeh, I'll bite. Why?"

"Yuh'd get your hand all wet an' smelly."

"Yeh!" Dutch cried. "That must be it!"

Had sauerkraut become Liberty Cabbage? Had Wilson run for President on the slogan *He Kept Us Out of War?* Dutch didn't give a damn. Germany to him was a map in a geography book. Were some of those German soldiers relatives of his father and mother? To Dutch they were as bloodless as the photographs in the newspapers.

They turned the corner of Forty-second and Ninth. Down at the foot of the street the Weehawken Ferry was like a halfway house between land and sea; its copper sheathing darkened into a dusty metallic green. As they approached, the smell of the sea became sharper. From between the barnacle-encrusted spiles a ferry was moving out like some gigantic watery monster, leaving a track of white foaming water.

Paulie waved his cap. "That's what I wanna be the

cap'tin of a boat like Georgie's ol' man!" he said all in one breath.

"His ol' man's just a guy what pulls up the iron gate to let the peepul on an' off," Dutch said with a sneer. "That Georgie's fulla baloney!"

After a while they left the ferry house. Without beginning or end, the day stretched before them, the horns and whistles of the freighters tootling, the gulls winged snowflakes in the sun. They watched dock wallopers at work, stared at sailors' togs inside the windows of the ship chandlers.

"Pipe that!" Dutch snickered, pointing at a drunken seaman arm in arm with a dame whose rouged cheeks were as red as the wax cherries on her hat. "How about it, Paulie?" When Paulie blushed, Dutch flung his head back and laughed. "What's the matter with yuh anyway? You never come with Georgie an' me when we see girls. You're scared! That's why yuh hang your head like a dope when yuh see Mary—"

"Shut your trap, I'm warnin' yuh, or—"

"Sorehead! What I'm tryin' to tell yuh, Mary's a good girl like my sister Gertie an' your sisters. See what I mean?"

Paulie understood him all right. There were good girls and bad girls, and it was a waste of time to fool around with the good girls. The good girls got married, and the bad ones ended up in the street. He was scared of girls, Paulie thought, they could be bad or they could be good like Mary. Scared, scared, scared!

Then, gradually, the waterfront like some three-ring circus pulled him out of himself. Ships like beached whales were being loaded and unloaded. Longshore gangs hooked up huge boxes inside corded nets. Whistles blew, some shrill as birds, others hoarse as if sounding out of the throats of strange beasts held captive in the holds.

Dutch hissed in Paulie's ear. "Cheeze it, the cops!"

Paulie stiffened when he heard him. No matter what the danger, cops or truant officers or kids with sticks from another block, you took off. It was kids this time, nine or ten of them, hookey players like themselves who had suddenly appeared from behind a canvas-covered hill. Huge boxes awaiting a gang of dock wallopers.

Two or three of them yelled: "Bastids! We'll mobilize yuh!"

"Cheeze it, the cops!" Dutch repeated the old Hell's Kitchen warning as he ran toward a side street, Paulie at his heels.

Faster than Dutch, Paulie shot ahead, veering sharply to get out of the way of a lumber wagon pulled by two horses. A whip lashed out and caught him on the shoulder, but in his fear it might have been a feather; he felt no pain.

Behind them, the shouts of their pursuers had thinned into whispers.

"Stop!" Dutch said at last. "Stop, we're inna clear!"

Panting, they wiped the sweat from their faces, drying their hands on the sides of their knee pants.

"Bastid micks!" Dutch muttered, and when Paulie said suppose they weren't micks, he glanced contemptuously at his friend. "Yuh wanna go back an' ask them?"

As they headed toward Ninth Avenue Dutch began to laugh at how they'd outsmarted those bastards, whatever they were, micks or chinks. He circled Paulie's shoulders, cooed like a happy baby. "Yep, 1-4-All, that's us!" He rubbed his belly when they passed a corner saloon: "Smell that lunch, Paulie! Pickles an' baloney! Yum yum, an' roast beef! Jeez, I could eat a horse."

Paulie looked up at the sun. It had a long way to travel before it was straight overhead, the noon whistles blowing, work stopping, school letting out, his lunch waiting at home.

Hungrier by the minute, they lingered in front of a bakery window where they played the game of what-you-would-buy-if-you-had-the-money. Peach pie or apple? Chocolate cake or jelly buns?

Maybe it was the bakery window, heaven on earth sprinkled with sugar, but Dutch burst out: "Yuh game, Paulie?"

"Game about what?"

"The peppermint building!"

Paulie couldn't believe he was hearing straight. The peppermint building, as it was called by every kid within five blocks of the ten-story loft on Thirty-sixth Street, belonged to the micks who lived in the house whose back-yard faced the loft. Up on the top floor they packed Life Savers of a dozen flavors, and when the workers felt good, they would step out on the fire escape and toss handfuls down to the kids begging for peppermints.

"That's a loony idear!" Paulie said. "They'll kill us—"

"They're in school—"

"S'pose they aint? S'pose some-a them's playin' hookey? Even if we was micks they'd kill us. Yuh forget that's why

they started that club o' their's, the 1-4-Alls to keep everybody out—"

"Ain't we 1-4-Alls too?" Dutch grinned.

"Yeh, an' who swiped that name?"

"Maybe we can swipe their peppermints—"

Paulie shouted, "Of all the loony idears!"

What harm was there in taking a look, Dutch argued.
And when Paulie shook his head, Dutch called him a
yellowbelly. Unhappily, still shaking his head like a dog
dragged along on a leash, cursing Dutch, he tagged after
him into the mick house, walking tip-toed toward the rear.
They stepped out into the backyard. Hanging from the
clotheslines, blue work shirts, pink bloomers, and blouses
bright as the flags of a dozen nations festooned the sky.
Dry, most of them, but a few dripped an uneven rain.

"The coast's clear," Dutch whispered.

Clear or not, Paulie felt trapped inside the two fences
enclosing the yard, staring at the sheds at the far end.
Behind the sheds the fire escapes of the peppermint building
ascended in black iron rows. They crossed the yard and
Dutch pointed at one of the sheds. Painted in big white
letters there were two words: KEEP OUT. Below the
warning, painted in black, a roster of names:

> G. Connelly, presadent of the 1-4-Alls
> F. Smith, vise presadent
> J. Riordan   R. X. Quinn
> P. Murphy   A. Dugan

Dutch spat at the locked door. Paulie glanced about the
empty yard as if he expected it to fill up in another second,

the black-painted names solidly fleshed, charging through the tenement door behind them, dropping down from the clotheslines!

"Fuck 'em!" Dutch said, his head tilting back on his thick neck, squinching up at the top floor of the loft. "Hey! Yuh got any peppermints? Peppermints! Peppermints!" he yelled.

Paulie shuddered and turned toward the tenement. Nobody looked out the windows. Unseen machines on the lower floors of the loft rumbled, clattered; iron tongues repeating the same message: *Cheeze it.*

"Got any peppermints?"

Listening to Dutch—no foghorn could've been louder—Paulie wished he was safe in school. A man in a soiled white apron stepped out on the top-floor fire escape. To Paulie he seemed suspended in space. He laughed and asked were they hookey players or something?

"Peppermints!" Dutch kept shouting like a wound-up doll deaf to human voices.

"Want peppermints, yuh gotta earn 'em! How about a li'l jig, yuh two monkeys?"

Dutch began to shuffle, then glared at Paulie. "Jig, yuh dummy!"

"Go to hell!"

"What'd we come here for?" Dutch screamed as if Paulie'd robbed him blind. "Jig, yuh dumb bastid!"

He hated Dutch, hated the man up on the fire escape, hated himself more than any of them as he broke into a hang-footed jig. Dancing like a monkey! And for what? A bunch of lousy peppermints!

The man watching them called to the workers inside the loft. Two or three joined him, and one of them tossed down a handful of Life Savers. As the two boys tried to catch the tiny wheel-shaped candies in mid-air—most of them shattering when they hit the ground—they roared with laughter at the free show; the fire escape like the box in a theater.

"Busted!" Paulie yelled wildly, kicking at the broken candy fragments. "Stinkers!" he cursed, shaking his fist at the faces in the sky.

"The li'l bum's a fighter," one of the workers jeered. "Look-a that fist!"

"Jack Dempsey the second!" another howled. "Hey, kid, show us how yuh train fer a fight!"

"G'wan Paulie!" Dutch urged, poking him in the ribs with a sharp elbow. "G'wan! They'll t'row us peppermints!"

"Shit on 'em!"

"Paulie, c'mon!" Dutch begged.

Feeling like a fool, Paulie raised his left arm, then dropped it. But with Dutch shrilling curses in his ears, he started to shadowbox. One in the gut, he thought, ramming a punch into the bellies high up on the fire escape. One on the button, he thought, smashing the knockout blow.

Through the clotheslines, peppermints descended like a wintry hail, white and gleaming. The two boys snatched them in mid-air, pocketing a few whole ones. As the men returned to work, Paulie and Dutch scooped up the brokens.

"Look what the cat drug in!"

They spun around to see a long, redheaded lank watching them from inside the entrance to the yard. He was leaning against the door jamb, filling the doorway like a cork in a bottle, not that he was one of those five-by-fives, It was the look of him, his face all hard edges, the twisted nose that'd taken many a clout. Hatless, his cropped red hair shone like metal, his eyes a rusty brown under red eyebrows. He was no stranger to either Dutch or Paulie. They had seen him sauntering along Ninth like a Tammany alderman as if he owned the street, yet he couldn't have been more than eighteen or nineteen. They even knew his name, for whenever there was talk of guys from the neighborhood who were Badgers, somebody would be sure to mention Red McMann. A tough gang, the Badgers, muscle boys and stickup men, and one of its toughest members was none other than the freckle-faced redhead you could spot a mile away, whose hair was so bright it looked as if a match had been put to it.

The two boys stared as if their eyelids had been pried open with toothpicks, not a word out of either of them.

Red McMann grinned, congratulating them on their brass-bound nerve. "That's okeh with me," he said. "I like kids with noive. Come along, yuh kids. I wanna talk with youse."

" 'Bout what?" Dutch asked in a shaky voice.

" 'Bout your ol' mother!" Still grinning, he told them to stop worrying. "Yuh think I give a shit for the stuff those cheap mutts chuck down? See, I was flyin' my pigeons up on the roof when I heard yuh hollerin' to beat the band," he explained. "How'd yuh like to see my pigeons?"

Dutch shook his head. Paulie, as if his own head were wired to Dutch's, shook his. Red McMann laughed and said they had nothing to worry about from him.

"I like kids with guts," he said, "so come along."

Afterward both Dutch and Paulie would agree they had smelled a rat. They shouldn't've gone with the bastard, but how could they have said no? The bastard would've polished the floor with the two of them.

The flight of stairs seemed endless to Paulie, the doors of the flats jiggling in sight like unsteady drunks, his hand sliding on bannisters worn smooth as glass by forgotten tenement generations. On the top floor an iron ladder led up to a square of blue sky. He climbed to the roof, blinking at the sun. Like a yellow sea it spread far and near over an empty expanse of tarred roofs and red brick chimneys.

Voices!

Paulie heard the kids hiding behind the trapdoor before he saw them, their outraged and furious voices promising bloody murder. Frightened, he forgot to breathe for a second. Tricked! he thought, gaping at the faces that'd surrounded Dutch and himself. None of them were strangers. Some of them were in his own class; others he'd known in the seventh grade, their names painted on the shed door down in the backyard: Georgie Connelly, the president of the Irish 1-4-Alls; Beanpole Riordan; Paddy Murphy.

"Get back!" he heard Red McMann shouting. "These two mutts came here to see my pigeons an' they're gonna see 'em!"

Paulie trembled at the laugh the announcement had caused. He watched the redhead squinting at the sky, watched him walk lazy-legged over to the roof wall where he picked up a bamboo pole. McMann raised the pole. No one moved; it was as if they had all gathered here to see how he handled his birds. McMann rotated the bamboo, the white decoy rag tied to its tip fluttering like a wing. Hypnotized by the white bird at the end of the bamboo, first one pigeon and then a second left the flock in the sky, alighting on the roof, folding their iridescent wings. The sun glinted on their breasts, and their green and purple feathers shone like ground-up jewels. The white bird moved toward the wire-mesh coop door. It was wide open. One by one, as if playing follow-the-leader, the pigeons stepped inside.

"Shut the door!" the redheaded pigeon fancier ordered. When it was closed he flung down the bamboo pole, grinning at the two peppermint raiders and their enemies. "I told yuh I'd bring 'em up. They're dumb, dumber'n pigeons!"

The Irish 1-4-Alls responded with a triumphant laugh, and then, as if recalling who the dumber-than-pigeons were and what they'd been up to, their faces hardened, their eyeballs moist and gleaming: the eyes of predators.

"Bastid crooks!" they shouted.

"Stealin' our peppermints—"

"Leave it to a fuckin' dutchman—"

"Yeh, an' that fuckin' polack, what about him?"

Paulie swallowed the choking spit of fear, the kids surrounding Dutch and himself blurring into one single figure emerged out of a nightmare. Anything could happen, he knew. They could be beaten to a frazzle, they could have their pants pulled down. Cockalized, he thought with loathing.

"Lemme at 'em!" Georgie Connelly talking, the president of the 1-4-Alls, his voice arousing a new outcry.

"Get back!" Red McMann shouted, and the howling kids retreated as if he'd waved an invisible bamboo. "Yuh guys!" he said to the peppermint raiders. "Yuh guys can't get away with it! Yuh gotta loin to stay where yuh belong!" His voice was low and implacable, a rooftop judge pronouncing sentence.

"They don't even live on this block!" one of the Irish kids yelled.

And a second: "Bastids come from Toity-eight'!"

"Shut up!" Red McMann commanded, glancing at the low roof wall. "I'm gonna give 'em a break. See that wall," he said to Dutch and Paulie. "If yuh don't wanna get lumped yuh gotta walk that wall. O' course yuh don't haffta, so make up your minds an' take your lumps like a man."

To Paulie the wall seemed as narrow as a skip rope. It was less than two feet wide; the brick of which it was made was broken in spots, and the mortar crumbled with age. His eyes shifted to the mob. One of the kids spat into the palms of his hands before knotting them into fists, another swung his haymaker.

"I'll walk," he heard Dutch saying.

"Yuh must be crazy!" Red McMann exclaimed.

"Dutch!" Paulie cried. "Don't walk, Dutch!"

He was jumped. An arm tightened around Paulie's neck, the kid with the stranglehold warning him to shut up. The roof tilted before his bulging eyes.

"Shut your ugly trap!" the kid hissed, easing the pressure.

The roof leveled out, and Paulie gasped as Dutch climbed up on the wall. He must have shouted or screamed although he was unaware of opening his mouth, the arm around his windpipe tightening. And again the pressure eased.

The redhead was urging Dutch to take his lumps. "I was only kiddin' about walkin' that wall."

"I'm gonna walk—"

"Goddammit, get off that wall!"

Dutch didn't budge, standing still as if cut out of the sky —the blue and beautiful sky of an hour ago, still blue but sinister, a blue hole.

Paulie screamed, "Don't!" and a fist thudded into his stomach.

"I'm walkin'," Dutch said, puting one foot forward. He stopped, raised his head as if he didn't dare look at the down-below.

Nobody spoke. It was as if they were all at some Barnum and Bailey circus eyeing the acrobats on the high wire above the three rings.

Paulie wrenched against the stranglehold around his neck, which instantly tightened. The boy on the wall and the spectators on the roof turned dark in his eyes, as if he were squinting at them through a blindfold.

Dutch slid his foot along the broken crumbling brick. His head had lowered, his eyes were intent on the wall as if nothing else in the world interested him, and breathing hard he hazarded a second step, a third, a fourth.

"Enough!" Red McMann broke the silence. "Enough! Yuh win! Get off!"

Dutch jumped to the roof to be greeted with clamorous

approval. The Dutchman was game! He was okeh! A humorist among the kids piped up: "Yuh can keep the peppermints, Yaeger!"

Red McMann himself patted the roof walker. Winking a rusty brown eye, he said: "Wun down, two t' go! Hey, polack, get ready to take your lumps!"

Pushed forward, Paulie stumbled. He recovered his balance and shouted, "Mick bastids!," raising his left arm, the fist clenched hard; his right hand lifted to protect his chin. Somewhere he heard Dutch, somewhere he heard the redhead, somewhere the Irish boys, but his own voice was far louder: "Yellerbellies! Why'nt yuh fight man to man?" He challenged them all, tears of rage in his eyes. "Man to man!" Mouthing words he'd heard a hundred times on the streets of Hell's Kitchen: the Irish code of fighting fair, fist against fist; no brass knucks, no clubs, no knives.

"I'll be damned!" Red McMann muttered as if reminding himself of what he had once believed in before becoming a Badger. "Okeh, polack!" Turning to the shouting kids, he asked who wanted to take the little bastard on, grinning at the volunteers. "The polack needs a lesson!" he declared and nodded at the biggest kid in the lot. "The polack's all yours, Paddy."

"That ain't man to man!" Dutch yelled. "He's bigger." Dutch was grabbed, silenced—an arm across his mouth like a wooden bar across a door.

Paddy stepped forward. He was half a head taller than Paulie, heavier by ten pounds. "Put up your dukes!" he said, winking at the audience. "I'll send'm home onna stretcher!"

Paulie waited, his left arm outstretched, rigid.

Paddy's upper lip curled in a prodigious sneer. "Scairt shitless, ain't yuh? Can't even talk—"

"Piss or get off the pot!" Red McMann said impatiently.

The bigger boy charged. Paulie jabbed with his left, danced back.

Paddy jeered, "Stop t'rowin' cream puffs!" Head low, his eyes two brown specks in his long-jawed face, he lashed out with his right.

Paulie ducked and felt himself pushed forward by unseen hands. A rock swung up out of nowhere, but it wasn't a rock: a fist. It smashed into his mouth. He tasted blood and spat it out.

Paddy yowled gleefully, "Wanna quit, yuh fuckin' polack?"

Paulie spat again, this time straight at the face before him.

Dutch plunged forward, and although still held by two of the Irish 1-4-Alls, managed to scream, "Thatta boy, Paulie!" before he was shut up.

Paddy wiped his cheek with the back of his hand, staring at the red stain as if he'd been marked by some plague. Silent and unbelieving for a second; then his lips split wide open: "Jus' for that I'm gonna moider yuh!"

Fists, so many Paulie couldn't keep track of them. He retreated, but the fists were faster. He backed away like an automaton who had been taught how to box—an exhibition that aroused a chorus of catcalls—his head clearing to see a single face. The others conjured up by pain had vanished.

"G'wan, hit me!" Paddy taunted, lowering his arms.

Paulie swung his left. Connected. Sprang forward. Gasped as if a hammer had driven a heated nail into his jaw; his arms suddenly too heavy, his legs too weak to support his weight, the tarred roof slippery like an icy sidewalk, the voices of the onlookers a steady roar in his ears.

He was unaware that blood was streaming from his cut lips or that he was staggering like a barfly who'd had one too many, jabbing with his left. It seemed detached from his shoulder, a mechanical arm propelled by some force that didn't belong to him. He was still hitting out with his left when he slumped to the roof.

"The winnuh by a knockout!" a faraway voice proclaimed. "Kid Irish ovuh the polack dummy by a knockout!"

That contemptuous voice lashed at him like the whip he'd felt earlier that day. His hands flattened on the roof. He managed to lift himself to all fours.

"Lemme finish'm off, Red!" Paddy pleaded.

"Nothin' doin'! The polack put up a good fight."

Quivering like a beaten dog, Paulie was unable to get to his feet. His eyes dimmed with tears at his weakness. With an effort he raised his head, his mouth opening, his teeth stained red with his own blood. "Mick bastids!"

Only those with sharp ears heard him, for his voice was the hoarsest of whispers.

FIVE

THE Badger office was wherever Spotter Boyle, the biggest man in the gang next to Clip Haley, hung his hat, a straw kelly in the summer, a derby after Labor Day. It could be Quinn's swell saloon with its genuine hand-painted oil paintings of nudes beautiful enough to dance in the Ziegfeld Follies; or it could be Cleary's joint, whose backroom was the hangout for any Badger with nothing else to do between jobs but play a little cards or polish his nails. That night the Spotter's derby, black as stove polish, every speck of dust brushed off, hung on a peg in the rear of McGowan's saloon on the corner of Fortieth and Ninth directly above the Spotter's head. A bony head whose temples and cheeks seemed to have been pushed in by a pair of iron thumbs.

Opposite him, in one of McGowan's private plush-lined booths behind the noisy bar, Red McMann was sipping his third boilermaker, a shot of rye followed by a beer chaser. With the booze tickling his funnybone and the business that had brought them together settled (a pawnshop burglary), Red McMann relaxed. He liked a good story as much as he liked flying pigeons.

"I'll tell yuh somethin', Spotter," Red began. "A real riot . . ."

And once again the freckle-faced redhead was up on the roof with the two peppermint raiders.

When he finished the Spotter shrugged. "So you got the dutchie to walk the plank."

"I didn' want him to. He could've fallen off! Jesus Christ, who the hell wants a corpse, not me, but the bastid! Stubborn! Like all these dutchmen. An' that polack kid! They were a pair! Yuh should-a seen the scrap he put up against a kid twice his size."

"I got nothin' else to do," the Spotter said.

McMann blinked as if the Spotter had reached across the table and smacked him one on the lips. "You're always sayin' we should be on the lookout for good kids—"

"All you were on the lookout for was your pigeons. Not that you're not within your rights to fly pigeons. Says so in the Constitution."

His voice hadn't changed. It wasn't sarcastic, flat and even, without any barbs, but McMann's pink face, pinker from the boilermakers, had flushed a deep brick red. That second he seemed like a kid in knee pants bawled out by a grown man who'd seen everything there was to see.

The Spotter was in his middle twenties, but no one in the gang could ever imagine him as being young. A queer one, no Hell's Kitchen boy like the rest of them, popped up from Brooklyn or Long Island somewhere with the story of an old miser who hid his money under his mattress. Johnny Burke, the Badger leader back then, had smelled something fishy. Who the hell was the long stringbean

44

anyway? He didn't talk like the rest of them. Lace-curtain Irish, not shanty Irish; but when they followed his pointing finger there was close to a thousand bucks under that mattress. The tip gave the Spotter his nickname and made him a bona fide Badger. And over the years the questions stopped. Johnny Burke was in Sing Sing; Clip Haley, the new leader, with the Spotter his right arm—and left arm too! Some of the Badgers complained, but only to a trusted pal.

"Okeh, I done somethin' wrong," Red McMann said, eating humble pie and not for the first time. "What, I dunno."

"Those two kids should've been beaten up and not let off the hook so easy."

"For some lousy candies?"

"It's not the candies. They had no right to be in that yard." Now that he'd made his point he said. "You know why I come down so hard on you?"

"No," was the honest answer.

"The Badgers got their foot-sloggers, just like the Yanks over in France. And the Badgers got what you might call officer material. Guys like you, Red."

The redhead was used to the Spotter's fluky way of putting things, but this was a little too fancy. "Me an officer? That's funny, but I see what yuh mean."

"About those two kids? What's their names?"

"Wagner, I think. No, that ain't it, somethin' like it though. Paulie, he was the polack."

"How old're they?"

"Fourteen or so, I guess."

"Keep an eye on 'em. Me personally, I don't give a damn what they are, dutchies or polacks. It was me who brought in Tony Ferrara and that Jew Joey Kasow. Clip squawked, but I brought 'em in."

McMann didn't know what to think. The pat on the back that'd followed the kick in the pants, the talk about foot-sloggers and officers, the lowdown about Clip and Tony and Joey. It all needed sorting out.

"Keep an eye on 'em," the Spotter repeated. "They look good. Maybe when they're a bit older."

McMann nodded his fiery red head. "Okeh," he said.

New kids were always coming along; some finished public school, but whether they graduated or not, the best of the lot ended up in the Badgers.

SIX

THEY made a little procession that June day after graduation—Paulie and Dutch, Georgie and Angie—the white tubes of their ribbon-tied diplomas reflected in the store windows on Ninth Avenue. Mrs. Bolkonski, Mrs. Yaeger, and Mrs. Alston brought up the rear. An uneasy threesome: Georgie's mother was too much of a la-di-da lady for Mrs. Bolkonski and Mrs. Yaeger. She walked as lightly as a skipping child; her girlish straw hat adorned with a waxen harvest of strawberries attached to the band. Mrs. Bolkonski's and Mrs. Yaeger's broad-brimmed hats were dark and funereal. Their step was heavy, as if their footwear had been soled with lead.

Angie's shoemaker father, Mr. Cuomo, the only father in the parade, grinning and joking, was like some field marshal. When he found himself lagging behind the women, he would bolt ahead, a perpetual smile on his lips. To him, the sunny avenue had widened into a world. America! the land of opportunity!

Mr. Yaeger and Mr. Alston were working as usual. Neither of them could afford to lose a day's pay. As for Paulie's father, he had been resurrected if temporarily by his widow's sighs. The shoemaker, himself a widower, consoled her in Italian. "God gives and God takes," he said, matching the woman's sighs with his own. Perhaps it was then—an impulsive man, Mr. Cuomo—the thought formed, an inspiration out of the blue summer sky, that they should have a graduation party.

"A part-y for da boys!" he cried. "Yes? We have-a da supper at my house! Yes!" he beamed, to repeat the invitation when they neared his shop. He shook hands with the three women and vanished in the ting-a-ling of the door bell.

The little procession went on, to stop once again at the tenement where Mrs. Bolkonski was the janitor and Mrs. Yaeger a tenant. The four new graduates rushed down the hallway. Mrs. Yaeger suggested that each of the ladies bring a dish to the party.

Smiling sweetly, as if a chocolate had melted between her finely molded lips, Mrs. Alston excused herself. She wouldn't be able to come. Please explain that to Mr. Cuomo. The two women watched her go.

Then, Mrs. Yaeger, her nose tilted, minced along the sidewalk in an imitation of High Society, all laces and furs. "So in her flat iss steam heat!" she exclaimed. "Who is she anyway?"

That day the backyard seemed different to Paulie, yet nothing had changed; the same clotheslines crisscrossed the yard, their shadows black cables on the ground. "No more school," he said unbelievingly.

"Yep, we're out!" Dutch declared, as if they were jail-birds who, after serving time, had been marched to the gates of the prison. He led the way to the row of sheds. "I'd like to give Ol' Dirty Drawers a kick inna ass!" He paused at the door of their club and kicked it (and Mr. Groteclose the principal), smiling at the others. "That dumb speech he made. Good citizens! Yah!" he mocked, his eyes narrowing as he glanced at the penciled marks on the door.

A week ago they had measured who was biggest with a 12-inch ruler fetched from P.S. 32 under Georgie's shirt. Dutch had elected himself the measurer, marking the five-foot spot with a heavy black line. That ruler in turn had rested on the tops of all their heads and Dutch'd penciled each of their heights on the door. Then he himself had stood, stretching his neck under the ruler. He was, as he'd known all along, the biggest—eight inches above the five-foot mark, beating out Paulie by a good inch. The two others no competition, Angie's measly five foot four topping Georgie by a shade.

Now, as he studied the penciled marks—another diploma of sorts—Dutch bet anybody who wanted to bet that he'd grow to six feet like his old man.

"Six feet in that fat belly of yours," Georgie laughed.

"Look who's talkin', the prize shrimp, an' he's older'n any of us!" Dutch retorted.

Georgie Alston was fifteen but seemed younger than the other 1-4-Alls, his face hairless. Black as a wop, the Irish never tired of reminding him; Georgie had often wished he had Italian whiskers like Angie. Angie's upper lip showed the faintest of mustaches; he'd be shaving soon. So would Dutch and Paulie; the golden down on their cheeks and jaws had thickened over the summer. Lately though, Georgie had stopped envying them. He had begun to feel that he was more of a man than the three of them put together.

"Yeh, I'm older," he said calmly. Lifting his hand, he wiggled his pinky finger. "There's more brains inside that finger, Dutch, than you've got inside your whole head."

"Horseshit yuh got inside your head!" Dutch jeered, unlocking the shed door. When they were all inside and the candle lighted, he produced an unopened pack of cigarettes. "No dinged-out butts for us today!" he grinned.

"Where'd you swipe 'em?" Georgie asked. "From your old man's pants?"

Dutch poked out his thick lower lip. "Want me to bust yuh one?"

"No fightin' gradjuation day!" Paulie shouted.

"Yeh!" Angie said.

"Paulie the big peacemaker!" Georgie laughed.

"Somebody gotta be!" Paulie said. "Ain't we been friends? So why fight now?"

Dutch nodded and passed around the cigarettes. They lit up, all of them silent as if hypnotized by the candle's little flame: a yellow eye focused on the gone years, one class after another, one teacher after another popping up like jumping jacks.

Dutch, puffing out blue smoke rings, said pensively, "We're out awright. Me, I'll get me a job, a good job."

"I'm gonna learn a trade," said Angie. "I'm gonna be a shoemaker like my ol' man, but no small store for me. I'm gonna work for some big Fifth Avenoo store an' get good wages."

"I've got to go to high school," Georgie complained. "All because my mother went to high school."

"High school'll be dif-rent," Paulie predicted. He was also entering De Witt Clinton High on Tenth Avenue, smiling as if he'd had a taste of the best lollipop in the world.

The doorbell of the shoe repair shop kept singing like a canary as the guests arrived to be greeted by the shoemaker, his son Angelo, and his daughter Mary.

"Thissa way," Mr. Cuomo said.

From the shop smelling of leather and shoe polish they walked into a kitchen in the rear where the marinara sauce simmering on the gas range blessed all their nostrils like incense in a church.

Mrs. Bolkonski had brought potato soup in a speckled black and white pot, followed by Paulie carrying a huge black bread. He was wearing his graduation suit, his legs in long pants—no more knee pants! no more black stockings!—and behind him Ava and Christina walked shyly, hanging their heads like yellow-maned colts.

Mrs. Yaeger's contribution was a round of beef in thick gravy, the vegetables tinted a mouth-watering brown. "Emil!" she shouted at her younger boy when he snatched a slice of salami from the table.

"Let-ta da boy eat!" Mr. Cuomo laughed.

Not in years had the shoemaker's kitchen held so many guests. The happy host poured a glass of red wine for each of the two women and for Mr. Yaeger, who stood solemn and gloomy in his Sunday blue serge suit.

"*Vino* like-a we say," Mr. Cuomo explained, and smiling he wished them, one and all: "*Buona fortuna*—good fortune!" To be reminded with his second glass that it was six years since his wife had died. A house needed a woman, he declared. Without a woman nothing was good. Then, in an abrupt change of mood he praised his daughter, Mary, who had swept the kitchen spotless and covered the two tables—one borrowed from a neighbor—with white cloths that could have graced an altar. Mary, he informed the company, was graduating from school on Friday. Smart, he boasted, an *A* student. He kissed his blushing daughter. "She's only thirteen, my Mary."

Mary had pinned one of the roses bought by her father from his friend Da Costa the florist in her long black hair, and if she wasn't a grown woman, neither was she a child. Boys existed for her now, no longer cutouts in caps, and if her eyes lingered longest when she glanced at Paulie no one—except Georgie—guessed her secret.

Munching on a green olive, Georgie sized her up. She was still skinny but her chest no longer looked as if a washboard had been slipped inside the white dress she had worn at her Communion. She was real pretty, Georgie thought, and shot the olive pit like a marble when no one was looking, watching it roll under the sink.

"Now we eat!" Mr. Cuomo announced.

There was a scraping of chairs as the four big people and the four graduates seated themselves at the main table. The four-not-so-bigs, Ava and Christina, Emil and Gertrude, with Mary as supervisor crowded the table borrowed for the party.

"First, soup!" the host said, then corrected himself with a laugh. "First, *vino!*" He refilled the wineglasses, and the conversation became lively.

"Wine, beer, *schnapps*," Mr. Yaeger affirmed, champing on a hunk of black bread washed down with a spoonful of Mrs. Bolkonski's potato soup.

Paulie glanced at Mary, who smiled as she urged the three little girls at her table to taste the olives. Warmed by that smile, Paulie felt like singing, the walls of the kitchen melting away into a dreamy landscape.

The kitchen itself had become transformed for all of them. Mrs. Bolkonski, sipping at her wine, forgot her sick body. She hummed a little Polish lullaby, and when questioned as to what it meant, smiled. "When I was a little girl, my moth-err—"

"Never mind!" Mr. Cuomo said. "Paulie a good boy like-a my boy. Learn a good trade, and my Mary she learn-a da type in high school." He reached across the table stained red from the wine and the rosy-gold flowers of marinara and patted Mrs. Bolkonski's hand.

She looked at him, looked at her son. "He go to high school!" she said in a strained voice. "Be some-bodee. No janitor like me."

"Somebody," Mr. Yaeger echoed, but there was no telling whether the pigsticker was optimistic or pessimistic. He helped himself to another glass of wine, his shaven face very white in the gaslit kitchen, his cheekbones flushed pink. "Somebody," he repeated, drinking, before voicing the motto that gave meaning to his own existence: "*Arbeit macht das Leben Suss.*" His wife translated: "Voik *macht* —voik id makes der life sweet like sugar."

Georgie felt like laughing. His eyes shifted to the little kids' table—the shrimps!—not seeing them, his eyes on Mary. He thought she didn't seem to belong to her family. Two of a kind, her old man and Angie, two black skinny hairy guys with skinny long pointed noses. Her nose was perfect, and there was no wire in *her* black hair. Even when he glanced away he could still see her face, round and rosy-lipped like the picture of the Madonna between the kitchen windows. A virgin Mary, he thought, until some guy cops her cherry; might as well be me, never be that dumb Paulie.

Georgie could have kicked himself if he'd had a third foot under the table. Here he was stuffing himself in her old man's house! Angie was his buddy! And Angie's sister, just like Dutch's or Paulie's sisters, was off-base. Christ, Georgie snapped at himself, weren't there plenty of Dirty Marys on the street?

SEVEN

THE 1-4-Alls had been Dutch's idea, and it was Dutch who gave the club the kiss of death. All that kid stuff! What did they need it for? Angie agreed with him one hundred percent, and Georgie said it was about time they sailed Paulie's pirate ship down the river. Paulie held out, only to have his arguments knocked down like a row of tin cans before a dead-eye slingshot. Sure, once they'd all worn diapers, Dutch admitted with a wink. And shit yellow, Georgie added. Yeh! agreed Angie.

Dutch rapped at the fruit-box table and blew out the candle, smiling at Paulie. "It's all your'n, pal."

Over the summer after graduation the 1-4-All leader had grown another inch, his jaw lengthening, no longer a moon-face as he happily observed whenever he peered into a mirror. Last but not least, the jingle of coins in his once-empty pockets separated him from the snotnoses who ran around without a thin dime among them. He'd gotten a job, a steady job, in September—no delivering pressed suits as he'd been doing all through steaming August—with Worts-man's Butter, Eggs & Cheese store on Ninth. It paid six bucks a week, a dollar a day. Four went to his mother, which left him two big ones; not a millionaire exactly, but it was a swell feeling to have some money of his own. When he broke a buck he liked to finger the change, particularly the big fat half-dollars.

Every morning, as soon as his father cleared out of the house, Dutch took his turn at the kitchen table. No matter how hungry he was, he always waited in the room he shared with his kid brother until his big pink-lobed ears caught the sound of the stairs groaning under the weight of that old man of his. He was more scared of his father when he sat white-jacketed and white-trousered in a fresh butcher's uniform than when he returned at night in the crumpled, bloodstained uniform of death itself. The reason was simple. Mornings, his father wasn't tired. Mornings, his father was as strong as the huge porkers he slaughtered. That old man of his, Dutch thought, was a pip. He could sit for hours on a Sunday reading his German newspaper, silent as a clam; and when he opened his mouth he always spoke in what he called the language of the old country—*Deutschland, Der Heimat*—the homeland. They ought to ship him back to that *Heimat* of his, Dutch used to think. What was so hot about it anyway? Wasn't old Kaiser Bill losing the war?

It was a relief to get out of the house. Downstairs, the fresh air, cool and crisp as an apple peeling, was a reminder that summer was over; and not only summer. A whole lot of things were over. He was no longer a kid. One of these days he'd be moving into a room of his own with no old man to worry about. He neared the corner of Ninth Avenue, grinning when he passed the window of Cuomo the shoemaker, at Angie working away. Glued all day to one spot, that dopey Angie. On Dutch's job it was always lively, the boss joking around with the customers, the boss's nephew Al at the scales, all of them busy as hell when the big rush started, cutting slabs of yellow butter, slicing cheese—Swiss, Muenster, and sharp tangy Wisconsin—Wortsman bringing out the Limburger and joking that maybe they should call it Liberty Cheese. Meaning no harm. That boss of his just liked to joke.

Dutch, his cap perched over one ear like the wing of some floppy bird, wearing his graduation suit, walked north on Ninth, the El overhead like a whirring alarm clock on wheels, screeching out a single message: *Work Work Work.* . . . The store opened at seven o'clock, and Wortsman had no use for sleepyheads. Now and then Dutch squinted at his reflection in the plate-glass windows with appraising eyes. It had become a regular habit, like the cigarette he lit up once he was down in the street.

What a mug, he thought. Those mick bastards had him pegged when they said he had a pig's snout. And squinchy eyes! Even his hair, he brooded, was too yellow, like it was painted on, not like Paulie's with its golden shine. He'd never be one with the girls like that weasel Georgie. Never! Not unless he had the jack to spend for a good time. A fat chance with his old lady latching on to four bucks out of his six.

Outside the cheese store the boss's nephew Al was waiting. "We're both early, Henry," Al said. (Henry was Dutch's name on the job.) "We gotta cool our heels. I heard a good wun last night. Dis farmer's daughter was milkin' the cows when dis salesman says, 'How many quarts d'yuh get?' She says she gets twenny quarts, and dis salesman says, 'Gee whiz, I'd never a-knowed it with the small tits you got.'"

Wortsman arrived as he always did, as if a wind were blowing his short pudgy body. He unlocked the door, and followed by the two clerks, marched into the stockroom. There, all three put on freshly laundered aprons. Spick-and-span as male orderlies in a hospital, Dutch and Al sprinkled the floor with clean sawdust, swept the sidewalk, and washed the plate-glass window. The first customer to enter the store received a sliver of Swiss, free, no charge, from Wortsman himself. "A liddle prezent," he said, smiling.

Dutch had to smile at what was a daily routine. He liked the boss, but his liking had never stopped him from taking home a quarter of a pound of cheese or so after knocking off work at the end of the day. He would've been indignant if anyone had accused him of stealing. What was a hunk of Muenster or Cheddar to Wortsman? The guy was rich, wasn't he, like all the Jews?

The busy hour began when the neighborhood women had sent their children off to school, the door opening and shutting nonstop, the counter two-deep with customers; the eagle eyes watched the scales for a cheating thumb; the pain-in-the-necks raised a hollar about old cheese or moldy cheese; the sniffers not only sniffed at the butter but also at the eggs, twelve sniffs to a dozen.

"The best, nothink but the best!" Wortsman proclaimed as he soothed the critics and made change at the cash register.

The register drawer had four clamps: one clamp for dollar bills, another for two-dollar bills, a third for five-spots, a fourth for tenners and anything bigger. That was a drawer and a half, Dutch (or Henry) had thought on practically his first day on the job.

When Paulie first saw De Witt Clinton High School he had been deeply moved, as if it were some kind of church. Like the church he attended every Sunday, Holy Cross on Forty-second Street. The high school occupied the entire block between Fifty-eighth and Fifty-ninth streets, red brick in its upper stories, faced with limestone; a flight of stairs like those of Holy Cross led up to the vaulted entrance, and when he climbed them, one in a crowd of hundreds, he felt as if he were the luckiest boy in the world.

"Gee, it's great!" he had exclaimed as Georgie listened with a little grin.

They met every morning, walking to school together. Their block, Thirty-eighth, was only a mile from Fifty-ninth.

To Georgie, going to high school was a waste of time. When Paulie asked why didn't he find a job then, like Dutch, he'd get the same answer. A waste of time! What was Dutch making at that cheese store? Six measly bucks a week! If everything was a waste of time, Paulie questioned one October morning, what wasn't?

"Anything I feel like doing," Georgie replied.

"Anyt'ing?" Paulie said, fascinated. "Like what, Georgie?"

"Like punching you in the nose, like robbing a bank!"

He half meant it, too, as Paulie realized. He stared at his friend's innocent choirboy face. "Nah, you're foolin' me again," he said at last. He couldn't believe, he didn't want to believe, that Georgie really meant what he had said.

But when the bell rang for the first class Paulie forgot about Georgie, forgot the streets of Hell's Kitchen, forgot the tough guys, the gangsters, the Badgers, the Hudson Dusters. Forgot that he always had a hundred things to do when he got home—halls to sweep, garbage pails to be hauled out. Forgot that he had no time to keep up with his boxing practice, too sleepy at night even to think of Mary Cuomo.

The bells rang in and rang out the classes—math, English, biology, American history—everybody dashing off to the next period in a Times Square rush. As week followed week the faces of his classmates emerged out of the crowd. The faces of his teachers became as familiar to him as his own. Mr. Kelley, his history teacher, was his favorite.

"I spell my name with two *es*," Mr. Kelley had announced at his first class. "We all have our little vanities and that makes us human. The great Americans we will be talking about weren't bronze figures but flesh and blood just like ourselves."

How had it happened? When, at what magic moment, had he fallen under the spell of Mr. Kelley's raspy snuffly voice sounding out of his eyeglassed face with its thick gray mustache? He would pace up and down, a little man in a baggy tweed suit, the living presences of the great colonials tiptoing behind him: "George Washington was a true democrat not because he'd been taught to be one but because he was a frontiersman. The frontier in his time was wild and unexplored and dangerous. The frontier was George Washington's school. Thomas Jefferson!" For a second the history teacher was speechless. "Whenever I think of Jefferson, boys, I am awed at his genius! He was an inventor, a statesman, but he had other qualities I admire as much. He had a great heart. Yet, like all human beings, he wasn't perfect. He was against slavery but he kept slaves, and yet in his time he was like the Statue of Liberty out here in the harbor...."

When Paulie met Georgie for lunch—they always lunched together—all he could talk about was Mr. Kelley.

"Kelley!" Georgie protested one day. "I'm sick and tired hearing about him!" And cocking his sleek head to one side he sang a variant of the "Kelly Song," as well known, or better known, in Hell's Kitchen than "The Star Spangled Banner."

> "Everybody here knows Kelly
> Kelly with the big big smile
> His hair is red,
> His eyes are blue—
> And he's Irish through and through"

They always ate at Miles Cafeteria on Tenth Avenue, a block away from the school. It was Georgie's favorite place, not that it mattered to Paulie, who always brought his lunch in a brown paper bag, a couple of sandwiches made by his mother. Georgie nearly always ordered hot dogs and baked beans. He would cut the frankfurters into even segments like so many miniature logs and then pour the catsup in a red rain while Paulie stealthily fished a sandwich out of the bag on his knees.

"Stop worrying somebody'll see you," Georgie had said a dozen times.

"I shouldn' be here when—"

"Jeez, Paulie, will you stop being so Goddam honest!"

"It ain't right."

"Is that what Old Kelley's pumping into your dumb head?"

"I don't buy nothin'—"

"So you don't!"

"It ain't right."

"If you can get away with it, it's right!" And raising his voice in order to be heard, glancing at the noisy eaters, the countermen dishing out green pea soup and half a dozen other ready-mades, he lectured Paulie on the difference between a guy who was a dope and a guy who wasn't. Dark eyes flashing like a terrier's, he never tired of the subject: "Paulie, you got a head on your shoulders like me, but you're full of dumb ideas."

"Our ideas're diff'rent."

"Sure, but where will yours get you?"

One day Georgie left their table to return with two slabs of chocolate pie. "My treat," he said to Paulie's questions. No, his mother hadn't raised his allowance; he'd raised it himself.

"How?" Paulie asked.

Georgie winked, and lowering his voice, he whispered that he'd looked around the locker room, and what do you suppose? One of those football players had left his dumb old wristwatch on a bench. Paulie stared at the chocolate slab of pie before him as if the swiped watch were inside it. He warned Georgie he was looking for trouble. Real trouble. Besides, it wasn't right; it was their school, their football team. Georgie grinned, picked up his fork, and scrawled a big *C* across the top of his slab.

"Georgie," Paulie pleaded. "Lissen, yuh think yuh can get away with murder—"

Georgie tilted his chair back on two legs, and raising his eyes soulfully to the ceiling, he began to sing one of the school songs: "When Clinton was the Governor in 1824 . . ."

"Shut up or I'll crown yuh one!"

Georgie nodded, gazing across the table at a blond stranger whose jaws and lips were clenched tight; so tight that the ordinarily smooth cheeks now had unnatural wrinkles. He felt no fear, only an intense curiosity. He thought that what people said about polacks was true. Wild, crazy! Sensible one minute and blowing their tops the next. "Crown your old pal?" he smiled. "You who didn't want to end the 1-4-Alls? Just because I think all this rah-rah stuff's a lot of crap? Never mind, pal. Old Georgie here carries no grudges. How about you and me stepping out Saturday night?"

Paulie shook his head.

"You're seeing Mary Pickford—I mean Mary Cuomo. Angie told me. Hey, what's the matter?"

Paulie's flush was so deep that his forehead below his hairline seemed painted pink.

Georgie took a bite out of his chocolate pie. "I can't

help liking you, Paulie," he said, meaning it, too. "But why I'll be damned if I know!"

Paulie again shook his head, and the motion seemed to loosen up his frozen tongue. "I like you, too, Georgie. Yuh can laugh your sides off but—"

"But what?"

"I mean— This is what I mean. I'd do anything for yuh or for Dutch. Or Angie. An' I mean it."

"I know you mean it. Dammit, Paulie, that's just your trouble. You're so fuckin' good!"

And that was exactly *why* he hated Paulie. He was stunned by the contradiction. He could understand the hating part, but not the liking. That Goddam Paulie was a real 1-4-All if there ever was one, working his ass off in school and after school, dropping by the shoe store Saturday nights to see Mary, and that's all he got out of it, a big see!

Georgie couldn't figure out how you could both hate and like a guy at the same time. Not that day anyway.

EIGHT

There was hardly a Saturday night when Georgie and Dutch didn't step out together. It might be a moving picture on Eighth or a game of pool at Milligan's. Best of all was when Georgie could talk Dirty Alice to meet them in the 1-4-All shed.

That Saturday night Georgie told Dutch about the wristwatch he'd swiped and dumb Paulie. "You should've heard him! Just like the Salvation Army!" He flipped his cigarette butt into the gutter and with it went all the preachers who had ever lived. "He ate the chocolate pie though," Georgie added thoughtfully.

"Why shouldn' he?"

Georgie glanced at his big hulky sidekick wondering if he should waste time explaining. Dutch wasn't dumb, his head wasn't just a hatrack, but neither was he real smart. Nope, Georgie decided.

The street had turned a dusky, nighttime blue, the globes of the lampposts lonely spots of light, greenish yellow like the eyes of monster cats. From off the river the wind, like a wild boy, kicked at a tin can in the gutter, booting the tag-ends of newspapers that rose and fell like stringless kites.

Georgie had sold the football player's wristwatch to a kid at school. "I could've got more than five bucks," he said with a groan as if he'd been robbed.

"Five bucks!" Dutch exclaimed. "I gotta work a whole week almost to make five bucks! But don't yuh worry! I get even!" he bragged. "Ain't a day when I don't bring some cheese home."

"Cheese," Georgie laughed. "All the cheese in the world won't buy you one single ticket to a moving picture!" And raising his hand in front of Dutch's nose he rubbed his thumb and forefinger together in the money sign.

"There's plenty dough layin' around that store, Georgie."

"Yeh, you've told me but—" Georgie paused. "You'd have to stick up the boss—"

"Forget that!"

"I forgot it. But just for fun, Dutch, how would a guy go about it?"

And as they walked toward Eighth Avenue, Georgie asking all the questions, the make-believe stickup was like a new game they played, batting it up and down between them.

"It'd be a cinch!" Georgie said in a voice so sharp that Dutch gaped at him. "I'm not joking," Georgie continued in that same sharp voice. Razor-thin, Dutch felt it scraping along his nerves.

"Yuh must be jokin'!" Dutch said.

"Hell, no!"

"Yuh better forget it!"

"Okeh, it's down the drain, pull the toilet chain." Georgie smiled.

Come Monday morning Dutch regretted ever mentioning the cash register with its drawer full of greenbacks. He was even sorrier when they went out again. All Georgie wanted to talk about was the easy money at the store. The stuff they could buy, the dames they could have. That night, before dropping off to sleep in the room he shared with his kid brother, Emil, he couldn't get that cash register out of his mind, the money drawer sliding out of the darkness, the stacks of green bills changing into girls, swell girls, no street-corner bums. He cursed Georgie, cursed his boss as if it were Wortsman's fault that he was tempted to rob him. An easy job, that it was. . . . Georgie was right. . . .

Every night before locking up, Wortsman would empty the till, putting the day's take into a brown paper bag like some kind of cheese to bring home to his wife. And the next day she would deposit the money at their bank.

"An easy job," Georgie kept buzzing like a horsefly. "The Jew opens the store when his bank's still closed. One of these nights somebody's going to hold him up and might as well be us."

"Forget it!" Dutch would retort.

Georgie would nod, grinning, "Okeh, you wouldn't know what to do with a real dame anyway!" And he would outline the full breasts and hips of a dream woman, tracing the shapes that haunted Dutch these chill autumn nights.

High school to Georgie Alston was a place, as he informed Paulie, where he could look around and see what was what. It could be a wristwatch begging for a new owner or a snatch of talk that maybe could be turned into cash. One morning he eavesdropped on a private conversation in his Spanish class:

"I tell you Doty's watching us."

"No, you just got cold feet."

That was enough for Georgie to begin snooping around. He discovered that the two boys he had overheard whispering belonged to the Textbook Squad. No one had to tell him about Doty. Mr. Doty was the unofficial police officer at De Witt Clinton, a Texan who remembered and emulated the old days of his native state with its roughriding sheriffs. He was a thin little man who made up for his short stature by wearing a bushy handlebar mustache as gray as his eyes. Georgie, ever since his theft of the wristwatch, like any lawbreaker had been concerned about the little Texan and his squad of students. They imitated (except for the handlebar) their faculty leader, as if they too hailed from the western plains instead of the sidewalks of New York. Tightmouthed, tough, they were known to the student body as Doty's Boys or Doty's Vigilantes.

In one of his free periods Georgie peeked in at the Doty squad room, which served both as lockup and court. Seated inside were four or five boys pulled in for smoking on the sly in the toilets or fighting in the classrooms.

"What d'you want?" the Doty Boy at the desk snapped at Georgie.

"Excuse me. I'm just looking around."

"Beat it!"

"Yes, sir!" Georgie smiled, and as he went off he thought, Yes, sir! and fuck you sir!

He hurried down a flight of stairs and a few minutes

later knocked on the door of the Textbook Squad. He entered without being asked and explained that he needed a new history book; his own had been stolen. As he spoke he glanced about the room. Books were everywhere, stacked on wall-high shelves, on the floor in teetering columns. A couple of boys were emptying a cardboard carton of newly arrived texts. He felt relieved that the two whisperers in his Spanish class were either in class or in the study hall.

"Gotta slip from your teacher?" he was asked.

"Yeh. Signed by Doty." He was smiling as if he'd cracked a joke.

Their eyes fixed on him. "You a wise guy?" one of the squad boys asked in a low, threatening voice. There were three of them in the room, and they now formed a semicircle inside of which Georgie stood.

"Better shut the door," he said.

The little circle contracted.

"Who the hell're you?" said the first boy.

"What d'yuh want?" asked the second.

"Some kind of bastard!" said the third.

"Take it easy," Georgie said. "I'm on your side. I was only kidding about Doty, but you guys better lay off—"

"Lay off what, you sneak?" one of them demanded, stepping close.

"Put a mitt on me and you'll all go to jail!" he warned them. Instantly, like a thunderclap that he and he alone had released, he saw that he'd caught the big stiff right in the middle of his crotch. Caught them all in the crotch. "I'm tipping you off! You better stop selling those goddam books!"

It was a guess, an easy guess, exactly what he would've

done if he'd been on the Textbook Squad. Before he left he had settled for a fiver, not much for a good tip, but not bad as a starter. Once the Dotys quieted down they had agreed, maybe in a couple of weeks, he would be cut in even-steven.

There were ten members in the squad, and before Georgie eased out he had said: "You can tell the rest I got a pal in the Dotys. . . ."

When he and Dutch met again, that fake pal was good for a laugh. "The only pal I got is nobody but me!" Georgie explained.

Big Dutch looked at him with admiration. Yep, he said, some guys sure had their nerve. What he didn't understand was who was buying all those school books. He'd heard of fences buying jewelry and furs—but books? Georgie slapped him on the back. There were all kinds of fences, he said. Chances were the books were being sold to book dealers out for a bargain.

They turned the corner and Georgie, patting the pocket where he kept his wallet, said, "With my fiver and your two bucks we got more'n enough for a good time."

Dutch quickened his step when they neared the line of people buying tickets at Ye Olde Drury Lane on Forty-second Street and Eighth. The movie posters attracted his attention. "Mary Pickford!" he exclaimed happily. "Her new picture!" Mary Pickford, Pearl White, Mabel Norman, Lillian Gish! the slab-shouldered boy was secretly in love with all of them.

He was disappointed when Georgie said. "Let's go to Broadway."

"For what?"

"For snot!" Georgie laughed, or maybe it was the easy fiver inside his wallet laughing. Those five bucks were springs in his heels. They walked to Times Square and turned north on Broadway where a million lights like gaudy stars pulled out of a dreamlike sky obliterated the night.

Georgie eyed the well-dressed men, arm in arm with their women. Five bucks, he thought, what the hell was five bucks and Dutch's measly two? He glared at Dutch, the big dumb bastard, and said bitterly: "One of these days your boss'll up your pay to seven bucks, maybe eight bucks, and you'll be rich!"

"What's eatin' yuh?"

"Some guys're too scared to piss out the window."

"Chrissake, Georgie! A stickup's too risky!"

NINE

It had been a long, long Saturday for Paulie, but that evening, as he wrung out the mop on the top floor, he was thinking that at eight o'clock he'd be seeing Mary. If only her old man wasn't so awful strict! But that's how the Italians were, watching over their daughters like eagle eyes. He'd be lucky if her old man said yes to taking her to a movie, and even if he did, Angie'd have to come along as the big chaperone.

Chaperone . . .

Georgie had tossed the word at him like a baseball. "Dump Angie! Get smart for once!"

Dump Angie? Fat chance!

Paulie sighed, murmured Mary's name, and delighted with the sound it made, repeated it. Sighed again, shrugged, and urged himself to get a move on. He whipped out the mop, its wet strands wriggling across the glistening floor boards.

A right to the jaw! he told himself. On your toes, Paulie! Keep your left up!

Right! Left!

He pulled the mop back. Were his fists clutching a

wooden handle? Yes, but encased in boxing gloves he threw out bone-crushing uppercuts, jabs, hooks.

Ladies and gents, the ringside announcer he had conjured up called out to the fight crowd. *The winner by a knock-out! Paulie Bolkonski the Polish Tiger! Champion of the U-nited States!*

Dipping the mop into a pail of clean water, he laughed at his pipedreams. If only he could begin training, real training. Someday, maybe—once his mother got her strength back. She was sick with something worse than the flu, but she wouldn't let him call the doctor. They couldn't afford it, she kept saying.

He worked steadily, floor after floor. He had two houses to keep clean now, 355 and 357. When the janitor at 357 had moved out, Paulie had rushed over to the real estate firm that managed the properties, Fenton & Hauser on Forty-second Street, and asked for the job.

Mr. Hauser'd felt his biceps and said: "I'll always give a hard-working lad a chance. You tell your mother she's lucky to have a son like you, Paul."

He had figured a way how he could take care of the two tenements. There were four upper floors and one ground floor in each house, ten floors in all. Ten floors and six days, skipping Sundays, to sweep, mop, and put the garbage and ashcans out on the sidewalk. Which meant that he had to do one and a half floors each day.

When he finished the top floor he emptied the dark gray pails of water in the hall toilet (one toilet on each floor served the four flats), flushed the bowl clean, and hurried downstairs.

It had been a long day begun early in the morning when he'd gone to Fenton & Hauser to collect his money, waiting in a crowd of mechanics, painters, plumbers, carpenters. He'd rushed home through Paddy's Market, the horse-and-wagon peddlers lining the curbs as they did every Saturday. He'd kissed his mother, slapping a ten-dollar bill and two fives down on the kitchen table.

The breadwinner of the family, his mother had thought sadly.

Later that morning Mrs. Bolkonski, with Ava and Christina as bag carriers, had left the flat for Paddy's Market while Paulie seated himself at the kitchen table to do his homework. Flipping open the pages of his texts he was utterly engrossed, saving his history homework for the last—it was his favorite subject. After lunch he'd kept a week-long promise to take his sisters to the zoo. Ava and Christina had laughed at the monkeys. When a polar bear extended a grubby white paw through the metal bars they had shrieked, clutching Paulie's hands. Calmly as any papa, he told them there was nothing to be scared of, his mind floating loose as the escaped balloons over the zoo grounds, wishing that Mary had been along with them . . .

Done! Through!

As he went down the stairs with pail and mops he imagined her old man saying: *Mary, you and Paulie go to the moving pictures. Me and Angie, we stay home.*

The fantasy took on dimensions. There he was on Eighth Avenue walking with Mary to the Arena, saying: *Do you want to see William S. Hart or go to the Drury Lane?* Down that same avenue, mounted on his trusty horse, six-shooters blazing, somebody who looked like William S. Hart, but wasn't, galloped after the band of desperados who had kidnapped the schoolteacher from the East, her blond tresses blowing in the wind, and changing into Mary's black hair. . . .

TEN

THE frosty air of October was like a hooker of straight whiskey that Georgie gulped down, filling him with a drunkard's barroom dreams of easy money. The ten- and twenty-dollar bills in Wortsman's cash register flew out to shape themselves into all the things money could buy. Freedom from school, freedom from home, a furnished room somewhere where he'd be his own boss. The only trouble was Dutch, singing out nonstop: *No stickups for me.*

As Halloween neared, the masks on sale in the stores— ferocious, grotesque, spooky—inspired Georgie. What about a couple of plain black masks to hide their mugs?

Dutch would have none of it. Masks or no masks, Worts- man could recognize him by his build and then, he, not Georgie, would be up shit creek.

"You've lost your nerve!" Georgie yelled. "I quit!"

He meant it, gospel truth, but over at Milligan's pool parlor, the ivories clicking, the losers paying off the win- ners, still another idea flew into his head like a winged greenback. Walking home with Dutch to their own block he faked a big yawn. "School for me tomorrow and the old job for you. Me with my mother nagging me and you scared stiff of that old man of yours. Hey, Dutch!" he exclaimed. "I got the answer to a maiden's prayer!"

"Okeh, I'll bite. Wot's the answer?"

Georgie warned him not to faint dead away. The answer was simple as apple pie. All they had to do was tip off the Badgers. Sure, they might come out with the short end of the stick, but what did they have to lose? A slice of that cheese-store money was better than nothing. Besides, it'd be a good way to get in with the Badgers. The gang was no longer one hundred percent mick. He'd heard that from a couple guys. There was a dutchman in the gang and even one or two wops and jewboys.

Dutch felt as if a street hydrant had opened up to let loose a torrent of water, knocking him off his feet. Now, even as he caught his breath, he had a foreboding that it was too late to back out. It never occurred to him to ask how and where Georgie had picked up all his information about the Badgers. That you could expect from a guy half-rat and half-weasel.

"Christ," Dutch groaned. "Why'nt I keep my big yap shut? Why'd I haffta tell yuh about that fuckin' cash register?"

"Okeh, I said nothing. You're not the first or last guy to settle down. Maybe your old man'll get you a job as a pigsticker same as him?"

"If yuh don't shut up I'll brain yuh!"

"Okeh, let's forget the whole damn thing! We're still friends."

When they met again on Saturday night Dutch couldn't squeeze a word out of Georgie as to where they were going. Three guesses, Georgie grinned. The Ziegfeld Follies to pick out a dame? The hoosegow for stealing a pound of cheese?

What the third guess was Dutch would never know, the second one had him hollering: "If you're takin' me to the Badgers—"

Georgie grabbed the big boy's arm. "Hold it! Hold it! Are you crazy? We're going to a saloon like you never saw in all your born days!"

They crossed Ninth Avenue, walked west toward Tenth, the blocks long and lonely; the yellow squares of the tenement windows seemingly unable to hold off the night.

"Here we are," Georgie said, pausing in front of a brownstone.

"This is one helluva place for a saloon. If you're trickin' me—"

He was addressing the back of Georgie's head. Georgie had skipped down a short flight of stairs to an iron-grilled door in the basement. His face a-grin, he called softly as he pressed a finger against a bell button. "My treat, Dutch."

Dutch was about to ask what the treat was when a voice sounded from behind the grille: "No punks!"

"We're friends of Charlie Ramsay," Georgie said.

"Why didncha say so?"

Dutch stared at the door swinging open. Heavy-footed as if a sack of cement was attached to his legs he tagged after Georgie, blinking at the smoke in the room they entered. A barkeep in a not-too-clean white apron stood behind a small mahogany bar fixing drinks for the customers: neighborhood boys all of them, dock wallopers in unbuttoned peabody jackets, clerks in stiff celluloid collars. They were seated at a dozen or so small tables mounted on braided wire legs. Dutch, trying to look older than he was, followed Georgie to an empty table along the wall on which there hung a painting that like some nighttime dream emptied his mind of all doubts and anxieties. He'd been wondering if this joint—only it wasn't a joint—was tied in with the Badgers somehow? And what was the big treat Georgie'd promised?

Dutch's eyes bugged as he looked at the painting. The goddess Diana with drawn bow was aiming an arrow at a deer half her size. She towered tall and voluptuous, rosy pink and creamy white, except where some customer had penciled the triangle between her thighs; the bartender had erased the pencilling, leaving the area a smudgy gray.

Only when he was seated did Dutch dare ask about the Charlie Ramsay stuff. Georgie grinned. They had to get in, right? Charlie Ramsay was the door-opener.

"Who the hell is he?" Dutch muttered.

"You know the cop with the big yellow mustache who collects the graft for the station house? You've seen him a hundred times on Ninth Avenue."

Yes, Dutch had seen Charlie Ramsay. There wasn't a week when he failed to breeze inside Wortsman's cheese store, to breeze out a few minutes later with a little contribution for some poor policeman's widow and her orphaned children. Wortsman would shake his head and joke that with every storekeeper on Ninth chipping in, that police widow must be rich as Rockefeller.

Yes, Dutch'd seen Charlie Ramsay. But leave it to Georgie, he thought, to know his name. "This joint's some kinda . . ." he whispered. "Ain't it?"

"I told you it was my treat. Next question! Where'd I get the dough?" Smiling at his own cleverness he winked at the fat face before him. "You didn't know I was a gypsy mind-reader, did you, Dutch? Remember what I told you about the Doty Squad and old man Doty? I sneaked in one day and swiped all their watches!" He laughed so loudly at his own joke that a couple of dock wallopers at a nearby table started to mumble about keeping kids out. The bartender overheard them and stepped from behind his bar.

"We'll have a coupla beers," Georgie said as the man approached.

"Oney got whiskey at four bits a shot!"

He had spoken loudly, and his audience laughed as if they expected the two kids to jump up and run for the exit.

"We'll have two shots," Georgie ordered. "What's money?"

The laugh, this time, was a rumble of appreciation. Only Dutch wasn't amused. Four bits! Fifty cents! He was thinking he had to work half a day to make that much money.

"I only got two bucks, Georgie," he whispered after the bartender had fetched their whiskies.

"Drink up, Dutch. This is my treat!"

Dutch hadn't touched his drink, but the handsome face opposite him wavered in his sight as if he'd downed a pint. And when he'd gulped the whiskey and followed Georgie into a parlor hung with mirrors, he couldn't help mumbling: "This is gonna cost plenty!"

"How many times must I tell you, it's my treat? Next time it'll be your treat!"

Dutch flinched. In the subdued light of the parlor lamps the cash drawer at the cheese store appeared for an instant. Even when it vanished he could feel it knocking inside his head. "So that's your game—"

"You want to beat it, Dutch? Beat it!"

Stiffly, Dutch sat down in a chair studded with red velvet nails, eyeing Georgie who, hands in pockets, strolled across the carpet. Sweaty, silent, he cursed Georgie for the tricky rat he was.

The door opened and a black-haired woman in a red evening dress stepped into the parlor. "What's this?" she exclaimed, her lips splitting in a contemptuous laugh. "Boy Scouts' Night?"

"We're friends of Charlie Ramsay!" Georgie answered, nothing boy-scoutish in his voice. He stood there, small, dapper, arrogant, his fine dark hair combed to perfection, his eyes fixed on the woman. "We're also friends of Spotter Boyle!" he threw in for good measure.

Friends of Spotter Boyle, friends in a pig's ass, Dutch was thinking. But Christ, he had to hand it to Georgie. Georgie was right. All a guy needed was a little nerve. The four-bits whiskey he'd drunk seemed to slide down his throat a second time, hot as fire, burning up all his fears.

The woman was smiling, no more wisecracks, as Georgie pulled out his wallet, the ten-dollar bill inside passing into her red-nailed fingers. "This way, gentlemen," she said

81

politely enough but with an edge of sarcasm. "This way—" to break off, whirling around in a fury to confront an innocent Georgie who had thrust the hand with which he'd goosed her into a pocket.

Dutch shuddered, expecting her to yell for the bouncer.

"You sure're something, aren't you?" she said to Georgie.

"You had it coming," Georgie said. "Now we're even."

"If you weren't friends of— Never mind, *mister*," she added with uncontrollable malice. "Go right upstairs."

Dazed, Dutch climbed after Georgie, his eyes on the carpeted stairs. A door slammed above him but he didn't hear it. Dutch peered down the corridor, the doors all shut tight as if nailed.

Not for long though. They had been expected. A rigorous if invisible discipline governed every move in this brownstone. One door opened, and a blond woman waved a bare powdered arm. Georgie hurried to her. Even before the door closed, a second door squealed on its hinges, and a second head, black-haired this one, on a powdery white neck appeared, her crimson lips parting in a welcoming smile.

Back again on the dark street Georgie confided that the blond he'd been with wanted him to meet her on her day off. "I told her I was too busy," Georgie concluded with a straight face.

Dutch howled with laughter. The street was dark but the mirrors of the parlor glittered inside his consciousness. Dutch was still in the arms of the phantoms of his dreams. And as they turned down their own block he sighed, "Boy, that was a real dame."

"You don't know what a real dame is, Dutch. A real dame's private stuff. Once I have my own place you just watch my smoke!" he bragged. "You can get a nice furnished room in Chelsea for five smackers a week and when I do I'll have me a nice little piece with the dew still on her!" They had passed the shoe repair store, the plate-glass window dark and not a light showing from the rear. "Speaking of nice little pieces," Georgie murmured. "That Mary now—"

Jolted out of his own fantasies, Dutch cried out in an outraged voice. "She's Angie's kid sister!"

"Jesus Christ, you're still full of that 1-4-All stuff! What're girls for, nice or not nice?"

"There's a limit, Georgie! Besides she's Paulie's—"

"Paulie's what? 'Cause he sees her Saturday night? 'Cause he sits around with her and Angie and the old man watching? Sure, that's good enough for Paulie. He wouldn't know what to do with a girl except hold her hand. The guy's still a kid. We're not kids, dammit!"

Dutch had pushed all thoughts of Spotter Boyle and the Badgers and Wortsman's register out of his mind. Swatted them away like a bunch of pesky flies. But now they were back again. "No, we're not kids," he said in a low voice that quickened, wild and reckless, in a second. "We're not kids!"

ELEVEN

"**P**AUL!"

In the bedroom adjoining the kitchen Paulie jumped from his bed as if his mother's voice had looped around his throat, pulling him forward with breakneck speed. One look was enough.

"Mama!" he gasped, rushing to the couch where she slept each night.

She tried to rise, fell back, and in his anguish the kitchen and everything in it seemed to breathe with a secret and sinister life—the cast-iron stove, black and menacing, its nickel trim glinting like the metal teeth of the giants in the tales he'd heard as a child on his mother's knee.

"Ava!" he shouted, tears in his eyes. "Christina!"

He put his arms around her shoulders, stroked her cheeks and forehead.

"Paul," she whispered.

"Yes, mama?" And without waiting for a reply, "D'yuh feel better now, mama?"

Invisible hooks had pinned her eyelids, but when Ava and Christina stepped into the kitchen she seemed to sense their presence. Slowly, she opened her eyes, and when the two little girls began to weep, she murmured: "Dry your tears. Rain comes from heaven." The faint smile that had touched her lips faded as if somehow she'd heard a voice that spoke to her alone.

Paulie shivered and in the Polish he seldom spoke anymore asked her what was wrong. She answered that it must be the influenza.

The influenza! the name of sickness! the name of death that had swept through Hell's Kitchen, through West Side and East Side, all over town, all over the cities, leaving a black track of headlines as large and ominous as those reporting the war: *The Battle of the Argonne . . . The Spanish Flu.*

"Help me get dressed," Mrs. Bolkonski whispered to her daughters. "You will be my maids."

Again her lips quivered momentarily in the tiniest of smiles. She waved her bony thick-knuckled hand—the hand of a janitor—at her son. He understood her wish for privacy and returned to his room. He pulled his pants on over his underwear, slipped into his shirt. He was so agitated the buttons seemed to melt between his trembling fingers.

He would never forget that morning, his mother slumped in the rocker, a fringed shawl around her shoulders. Ava and Christina had combed and brushed her long hair but they hadn't managed too well with the bun at the back of her head. It dangled loosely, and Paulie, peeking at it now and then, was sickened by the thought that his mother had come apart like some oversized doll. Yet, when she spoke her voice was clear, her instructions precise and not to be disputed.

"Yes, mama," he said, lighting the gas range. He fried

eggs for his sisters, sliced bread, poured tea, and sent them off to school after writing notes to their teachers, explaining why they were late.

They had kissed her tearfully, and smiling a little, she dabbed her forefinger in a tear rolling down Christina's round pink cheek. "What diamonds tears could make!"

When the girls were gone she told Paulie that now he could telephone Dr. Reich. "Go!" she said when he hesitated to leave her alone. "The Devil will not take me."

He grabbed his mackinaw and cap, shut the door he'd painted yellow, the yellow of flowers and wheat—and ran down the corridor to the vestibule. Prayers, like soap bubbles, formed and broke in his mind, one after another.

A windy rain was falling in the street. He didn't feel it against his cheeks, blind to the rain-streaked tenement walls, the slate sidewalks polished clean and black.

There was a telephone in the store on the corner—Hazelkorn's Department Store—a poor man's miniature of the great establishments, Macy's and Gimbel's, on Herald Square. As he entered, Mr. Hazelkorn walked toward him between counters piled with kitchen wares and dry goods.

"Who's sick dis time?" the man asked sympathetically.

Paulie didn't see the chubby face before him, the black-buttoned sweater bulging over a pot belly. "Mr. Hazelkorn, it's my mother! I gotta call the doctor an' I forgot the nickel to pay for the phone."

He was told to keep his nickel. Lifting the receiver from its hook, he gaped for a second at the black collar encircling the mouthpiece: a strange and magical instrument that joined the voices of the near and far. The only calls he had ever made were to the family doctor. He licked his lips, gave the operator Dr. Reich's number, and listened to the ringing inside the receiver pressed tightly against his ear; the entire lobe had reddened from the pressure. He started at the answering voice, a woman's voice, disembodied.

"It's my mother—"

"What's her name."

"Mrs. Bolkonski."

"Spell it out, please."

He spelled the name, gave the address of the house where they lived. "My mother's awful sick, ma'am. Please tell Dr. Reich right away, please...."

Shortly before eleven Dr. Reich arrived. He patted the boy's head, smiled at Mrs. Bolkonski, put his dripping umbrella in the sink. "Well well well," he said, getting out of his coat.

His coat was black, his felt hat was black, his stringy tie under his celluloid rain-spotted collar was black, his mustache was black. When Paulie was a child the tall, stoop-shouldered doctor had been as frightening as a bogeyman. But he was no longer frightened, nor were his two kid sisters.

Night or day, rain or shine, Dr. Reich never failed to respond to a call. He was blessed by every mother with a sick baby, respected by good folk and bad. The word was out all through that section of Hell's Kitchen: *Yuh can stickup your ol' man, yuh can stick up your ol' lady, but steer clear-a that dutch doctor unless yuh wanna end up inna morgue.* Dr. Reich was an Austrian Jew, he could've been a chinaman and walked safe on those gaslit streets guarded by an invisible escort of Badgers.

"It is not the influenza," Dr. Reich said after completing his examination and locking his black bag. He tapped the couch with his long-fingered hand. Mrs. Bolkonski, he declared, must stay in bed all day. Tomorrow she was to go to St. Mary's for a blood test. "I will telephone the clinic, Paul. Today—today is Tuesday, *ja?* Thursday I will be here." And picking up his umbrella, his black felt set squarely on his head, his black coat collar raised, he passed through the door as noiselessly as a storybook magician.

Wednesday morning Paulie and his mother left the house. St. Mary's, on the corner of Thirty-fourth and Ninth, was a short walk from their street—four blocks—but they had to stop a dozen times; and at each stop he prayed to Jesus to give his mother strength. He prayed when they walked into the clinic that smelled of ether and the unwashed who, like humble schoolchildren, sat on the long wooden benches.

He prayed when he was alone.

His mother smiled wanly when she rejoined him. "They took my blood in little bottles," she whispered.

She was even more exhausted going home, leaning heavily on his arm, the stops more frequent. Once inside the flat she hurried to the couch and collapsed, too weak to raise her legs. He lifted them, tears in his eyes to see her so helpless.

"Sleep, mama. Sleep, mama."

"Go to school," she whispered.

"Not today, mama."

"My big nurse . . ."

He stayed home the next day, his textbooks on the table unread. He sprang to his feet at the doorbell. Dr. Reich, dressed in black as usual, entered. The rain had stopped, the curtains of the kitchen windows stained a brilliant gold. In the clear blue sky above the backyard a sun yellow as a Halloween pumpkin had sprouted on a stem of drifting clouds. The doctor smiled and asked him to leave the kitchen. Paulie sat down on his bed. With the door closed it was dusky night in the hall bedroom. So dark that the holy pictures of the saints, bright as house paints when seen in light, were grayish; the thorn-crowned Christ, King of the Jews, a funereal figure.

"Dear Jesus, Son of God," he prayed. "Save mama."

When Dr. Reich called to him he walked into the kitchen like an old man. And like an old man he listened to what was said to him.

"Your mother has leukemia, Paul."

On and on the doctor spoke, but Paulie scarcely heard him. And when he was alone with his mother, neither of them could remember the name of the disease.

"A disease of the blood," she said. "A disease of the blood—white blood—but how can blood be white?" Frowning, "Where is my memory? A name like the name of the blessed Saint Luke. . . ."

Even Georgie, the know-it-all, had no answer. On the El to school—the rains, which had returned, were beating against the rattling windows—Georgie suggested that if he was so worried about this white blood thing he ought to telephone the doctor. They hurried down the flight of El stairs, walking toward the high school looming before them in a bluish mist.

Paulie shook his head. "He says she gotta rest, so what's the diff'rence what the name is?"

"The difference is you want to know. Call your doctor! Don't be so damn shy!"

Before he went home that day, Paulie telephoned Dr. Reich: "Shouldn't blood be red? So how can my mother have white blood?"

"The blood is made up of red and white blood cells, or leukocytes."

"An' they're white?"

"They're colorless. Their function is to fight infection, but when there's no infection, they keep producing in great numbers—that's abnormal, Paul." A fatal disease, leukemia, but Dr. Reich couldn't bring himself to divulge that fact.

Overwhelmed by what he'd learned, Paulie stared at his pink-skinned hands, visualizing his mother's not as they were, but white as snow and lifeless.

"Your mother isn't better, but she isn't worse," Dr. Reich assured Paulie and his two sisters on his next visit. He patted little Christina's head, glanced at Mrs. Bolkonski sitting in front of the glowing kitchen stove on which a pot of potato soup was boiling, asked who was the cook, and when told, congratulated Ava. "A good soup is the best part of a meal," he smiled.

"Doctor, take your coat off," Mrs. Bolkonski invited him. "Have some soup, yes? It's so cold today."

Only now did the doctor explain why he'd dropped in. "I want you to see a specialist, Mrs. Bolkonski. I have spoken to Dr. Stenson," he said, writing the specialist's name and address on his prescription pad. "Dr. Stenson knows you cannot afford to pay much. He is a good man." He smiled at the sick woman and her son, for clear as clear could be, their eyes asked the same question. "It will cost four dollars."

Paulie couldn't sleep after the visit to the specialist's office. Like a jumping jack, the figure of Dr. Stenson kept popping out of the dark box behind his closed eyelids. He groaned, opened his eyes. The door to the kitchen where his mother slept was ajar. He couldn't see the kitchen stove, but the glow from the burning coals was like a radiant rug. *Leukemia*, Dr. Stenson was saying once again after leading Paul into another room where they could talk in private. *Leukemia is a fatal disease, my boy, and since you have no father, you must know the truth. When your mother's condition gets serious, she will have to go to a hospital.* Sleeplessly, he confronted the ghostly face of the jumping jack, a ghost himself haunting the spook house his bedroom had become. *Can't we take care of her at home?* Paulie was saying, tears in his eyes. *Yes*, came the answer, *if you can pay for a private nurse....*

"I'll find a way," Paulie muttered out loud, repeating what he'd said to Dr. Stenson. Wasn't he making twenty bucks a week? And frantically he figured that if they cut down on food a little, they could keep their mother out of a charity ward. Coal, gas? Couldn't save much there. And if Ava or Christina got sick? Nah, they're healthy kids, he thought. A nurse, though, was expensive. Fifteen or twenty dollars a week, the doctor had said. But plenty of women in the neighborhood would work for a lot less. Work for a dollar a day, or maybe a dollar and a quarter. "I'll find a way," he promised himself, his eyelids drooping, the rosy light in the kitchen spinning like a juggler's saucer, faster and faster, darkening by the second. His lips moved soundlessly as the great round of sleep finally carried him away.

The news of Mrs. Bolkonski's sickness spread through the house, and if some tenants offered nothing but pity— "Didja hear? What a shame? An' with Thanksgivin' comin' an' Chris'mas round the corner!"—scarcely a day passed when some lady or other didn't knock on the janitor's yellow door to bring a dish of cold meat or homemade applesauce. Mrs. Yaeger trudged down the stairs bearing a steaming pot of chicken soup with noodles. Mr. Cuomo the shoemaker called with his daughter Mary, a bottle of *vino* in a paper bag, his eyes shining with an invincible belief that wine and wine alone was the best of all medicines. Mary quietly questioned Paulie. When they left Paulie stared for a second at the closed door, as if Mary's face like a colored decal had been transferred to the wood.

Maybe it was the trip to the clinic, or the doctors' visits, but his mother seemed to get a little better. On Sunday she was able to go to Mass as usual, the whole family in their Sunday best walking down Ninth Avenue to Holy Cross Church on Forty-second Street. They ascended the creaking wooden stairs to the U-shaped gallery and sat down among the other worshippers, wrapped in the peace of Sunday as if in a lamb's soft robe.

After a while Paulie became aware of the priest speaking about the war in Europe and the soldiers fighting there, boys who had been baptized in Holy Cross. He listened, his eyes shifting from the priest's earnest young face—it was Father McGinley—to the altar boys waiting inside the entrance to the altar. The priest began to pray in Latin; the mysterious and holy tongue rolled time away, and when Paulie knelt to partake of the bread and the wine, the body and blood of Jesus Christ, he thought of the Sunday Masses when his father had been alive and his mother had been strong and well. He wiped a tear from his eyes and then felt himself flooded with a great happiness, as if he had entered some sanctuary

And when he walked home with his mother and sisters, the streets of Hell's Kitchen, too, seemed washed clean in the blood of redemption; there was no sickness in the world, no grief, no violence.

PART TWO

THE BADGERS

How did the Badgers get their name?
Nobody knew for sure. Some said that
back in the old days, before Clip
Haley was the leader, before Boxcar
Johnson, before Johnny Burke, before
Red Halloran, and before even him,
the Badgers got their name by beating
up cops and taking their badges.

TWELVE

"**H**ow-do, boys," Spotter Boyle said politely as he glanced up from the side booth at Red McMann who'd personally conducted Dutch and Georgie into the backroom of Quinn's saloon on Eighth Avenue; leading them past the bar with its lineup of tipplers and busy bartenders who, inspired by the nearness of Christmas, were smiling like Santas.

"Sit down," said the Spotter.

Noiselessly, as if there were greased steel springs inside his long shanks, the freckle-faced redhead slid into the booth alongside the Spotter, grinning as he listened to the initiation. For that's what it was. The two kids were as good as in, even if they didn't know it.

The Spotter, a deadeye dick for memory, hadn't forgotten the story of the little rooftop fracas with the dutchie doing a tightrope on the very edge—the backyard six stories below, and curtains if he slipped. "Yeh, it's the same dutch kid," McMann had informed the Spotter. Nor had the Spotter forgotten the dutch kid's pal, who'd taken on a kid twice his size and been beaten into pulp. "The polack's a mama's boy," McMann had replied to the Spotter's questions, and scratching a chin hard as a baseball, he had mused: "Wait'll yuh see the limey. If there ever was a cold fish . . ."

"There must be some law about minors," the Spotter remarked to the two kids on the other side of the table, the thinnest of smiles on his face. "And I don't mean coal miners."

It was a set speech of his, delivered whenever he met up with young punks fresh out of diapers but hot in the pants to join the Badgers. The Spotter was in his middle twenties, the old man of the gang, and there were days when because of that bum heart of his, he felt he was edging a hundred. He was thinking that the two kids sure made a cockeyed pair. One as blond as the other was dark, the blond boy big enough to lift a piano and the shrimp almost small enough to join Singer's Troup of Acting Midgets playing at Loew's American. The limey was pretty as a girl; the dutchie had a face only a mother could love, and that providing she was blindfolded. McMann had filled him in on all the dope he needed to know. A cheese store on Ninth owned by a Jew by name of Wortsman who every night took the day's cash receipts home to his wife in a paper bag.

The Spotter's sunken eyes shifted to the dutchie. Big Boy was a little skittery, the Spotter thought. It was a hundred-to-one shot he'd never been inside a swell saloon like Quinn's in his whole life. Neither had the little limey, which didn't stop him from acting right at home.

In the nearby booths women with rouged faces, dressed like peacocks, their long skirts brushing the gleaming hard-wood floor (Quinn's was no sawdust-covered joint), sat drinking with their escorts. Cigarette and cigar smoke veiled the faces of the backroom patrons, dulling the jeweled stickpins in the neckties of the men, smoothing out the wrinkles of the women.

Motioning to a waiter, the Spotter announced that it was his treat. Red McMann ordered a boilermaker, a shot of rye with a small beer for a chaser.

Before the words were out of Red's mouth, the baby-faced limey said, "Make it two."

"Beer," Dutch said nervously.

Georgie's *make it two* had rung unpleasantly in the Spotter's long, flat ears. He was certain now that the limey, for all his sugar-candy looks, was too cocky for his own good. He was the one who'd come running to McMann with the cheese-store tip although the dutchie was the one who worked there.

"How old're you?" he asked Georgie.

"Sixteen."

"An' now you're ready to vote?"

"I'm ready for anything."

The Spotter had heard that line before from other punks tooting their own horn. No harm in it most of the time. Noise never made a wheel go. But the limey was more than noise. There was a brain, a real brain, behind those spaniel eyes. Not that the dutchie was stupid. Real brains, though, was something else, and the Badgers had all they needed. His own. Suddenly he didn't like one single thing about Babyface. Not his looks, his brass, his funny way of speaking. Out-of-town, he guessed. "Where'd you learn to speak the King's English?" he inquired with a smile, pleased when the limey was taken aback. "You deaf? Where the hell d'you come from?"

"Massachusetts."

"A foreigner!" the Spotter said to Red McMann, whose shaven lips fitted together in a stony line split into a grin. "We're wastin' time," the Spotter continued, and over their drinks—he had ordered a beer because on doctor's orders he'd given up the hard stuff—the job was discussed.

He had to put the clamps on Babyface. "You his lawyer," he jeered with the honest contempt of a born crook for the legal profession. "You, Dutch, speak up! I'm not goin' to jump down your throat." Now and then he interrupted with a question. "Might be a couple of hundred in the till," he said finally. "Maybe double on Saturday night. Okeh, when this Wortsman guy goes home to his missus, we'll lighten his load." An easy job and not to be sneezed at, he was thinking.

It was lean and hungry times for the Badgers and for gangs all around the town. A little burglary, a little gambling, a floating crap game in some flat. And although the Spotter had his scruples, he wasn't too proud to turn up his nose at a little pimping. Better times were coming if Quinn were to be believed. The saloonkeeper, unlike most saloonkeepers, wasn't worried about Prohibition.

"Ostriches!" Quinn had said to the Spotter in many a private confab in an Irish brogue so thick you could serve it as soup. "They keep sayin' this Pro-hibishin ain't possible even with one benighted state after another votin' dry. You listen to me, Spotter, me bhoy. Pro-hibishin or no Pro-hibishin, nobody's goin' to stop a free-born Amurrican from drinkin'. If it ain't legal it'll be illegal. Sure, I'll have to close my saloon, but I tell you this Pro-hibishin'll turn out to be a gold mine."

The Spotter, too, was more than willing to squeeze a buck out of the great American thirst. Which was one reason why he was recruiting guys left and right for the Badgers.

He nodded at the two punks Red McMann had brought in. "What d'you think your tip's worth?" he asked. "Not you, Georgie. I'm talkin' to Dutch here."

Rubbing his moist palms on his pants under the table, Dutch wished once more that he'd never listened to Georgie. The Spotter's eyes had fixed on him; the pupils, grayish blue in color, had no more expression in them than the hard-boiled peeled eggs over at the bar. "Whatever yuh think's fair," he said.

"How about ten bucks for you an' ten for Babyface?"

"We ought to get a percentage," Georgie spoke up.

"How about fifty-fifty?" the Spotter smiled.

Georgie grinned. Fifty-fifty was too much. The Spotter agreed. Twenty percent was too much; after all they were minors and wouldn't know what to do with so much money. Tapping the table with his long bony fingers, he declared that nobody'd ever said he wasn't generous. If the job came to four or five hundred, the tip was worth twenty bucks a man, and besides the money he was ready to take them into the Badgers. "On probation," he added.

"On probation!" Georgie exclaimed.

"You heard me, but since Christmas is comin' "—his eyes lifted toward the smoky ceiling like a saint—a saint gone bad and a little moldy at the edges—"I'm willing to bend over backward. Bring in some more tips like this one. Where these storekeepers keep their dough. When they take it to the bank or whatever. Get me?"

"You're asking for the sky," Georgie said unhappily.

"Kiddo, I wish I could break the rules for you and Dutch. If it was up to me I'd take you in in a minute. But rules're rules!"

No one except Dutch was fooled by that declaration. Red McMann, lighting a cigarette, couldn't figure the Spotter. There were no rules, there'd never been any, and why the Spotter was putting these two kids through the meat grinder was beyond him.

"You, Dutch," the Spotter called. "Why so mum? What do you think? Speak up! You got a right. Says so in the Constitution."

"Me? I work for just this one guy. I don't work for the whole Nint' Avenue!"

"I know that, kiddo. But if you don't like it we'll forget the whole thing—"

"We'll figure out something," Georgie said hastily.

The Spotter congratulated him. He had the makings of a real Badger, yes, sir.

Afterward, when the two kids had left the saloon, he explained why he was sweating blood out of the pair. "It's that limey, Red. A foxy bastid if there ever was one. Nobody's smarter than a smart limey. How else could they keep the micks under their bloody heel—and not only the micks, half the world. The bloody bastids! Top dogs with the sun never settin' on their bloody flag!"

High-faluting talk to Red McMann who for the life of him couldn't see much connection between the little limey and the British Empire. But one thing was sure. He wouldn't want to be in little Georgie's shoes, not with the Spotter so steamed up.

"We got to play it safe," Georgie told Dutch after the stickup of the cheese-store owner. "You can't quit your job, and I can't quit school—not until the cops cool off."

That furnished room still seemed as far away as ever, but as Georgie assured Dutch, he wasn't asleep at the switch. "Don't you worry, I'll figure out something. That lousy Spotter will have to take us in."

THIRTEEN

Father McGinley's frown deepened as he listened to the blond boy who, like so many others, had sought him out in his office in Holy Cross Church. They came, they came, the priest meditated sadly, each bearing his own cross.

Except for a desk and chairs that might have belonged to a lawyer or a businessman down on his luck, the office was as austere as a monk's cell; the buff-painted walls bare except for a three-foot crucifix.

Gently he questioned the boy, and as he fitted the pieces together of a puzzle to which there was no real solution, his lips tightened. As if recoiling from a world in which there was no end to suffering. A rugged man, Father McGinley, with the athlete's shoulders of so many young Irish priests, but he still hadn't grown the muscle to ward off the misery of his parishioners.

"Let me get it straight, Paul. So far your mother, thank God, does not need a nurse. But if she does, how will you be able to afford it? Even if some neighborhood woman stays with her while you and your sisters are at school, that would cost a dollar or a dollar and a quarter a day as you've told me—"

"My mother's not gonna go to any charity hospital!" the boy interrupted quietly enough but there was a suppressed passion in his voice that caused the priest to raise his hand to his brow. He held it there like a protective screen.

"You earn twenty dollars a week, Paul," he reminded the boy. "Your only relative, your uncle in Chicago, is a poor man."

"He promised he'd help an' he will. We brought him over to this country. I mean, when my father was alive, he sent my uncle money for the steamer ticket. Here's the letter he wrote." He dug his hand into his pocket and pulled out a sheet of blue-lined paper.

The priest took it, unfolded it, and glanced at what the boy's uncle had written. "Your uncle is a good man," Father McGinley said, returning the letter. As the boy reached for it, he once again noticed the reddened knuckles and ruined nails: an eloquent witness, that hand, to long hours of labor. "Paul, do your grades at school suffer?" he asked.

"Suffer?"

"You can't have too much time to study."

"My grades're okeh, Father."

"May I ask what they are, Paul?"

"Last markin' period I got all *A*s except for a B in French."

"That's wonderful!" Father McGinley exclaimed. His interest quickened. "I wish I could help you," he said, sighing as he opened a drawer in his desk. Inside there was a gray metal box (the "poor box" the priests at Holy Cross called it). Flipping the cover, he took out five dollar bills. "It isn't much—"

"Thanks, Father, but I don't need it."

"Paul, your twenty dollars a week's no fortune with four people to feed and clothe and money for doctors and medicines."

"Honest, Father. We're all right—"

"You don't like charity, do you?"

Paulie was silent: a silence that seemed to echo in the office: *No, I don't like charity.*

The priest frowned. "Let me think. I could get you part-time work with one of our parishioners, but you've got enough work as it is."

"I could fit it in!"

"When, Paul? After midnight?" He smiled at his little joke.

"But I could!"

"Are you sure?"

"Yes, Father."

"Very well then. I'll speak to Mr. Duffy."

"Duffy!" Paulie grimaced.

"Do you know him? Mr. Duffy the painter boss?"

"I don't know him."

"Then what's the matter?"

"He mightn't want me."

"Why not?" He stared at the boy who sat there, his head lowered, his eyes downcast. "I see! Because you're Polish?"

"Yeh," Paulie muttered.

Father McGinley laughed. "I'm Irish, Paul. Mr. Duffy's a good man, a good Catholic."

"Yeh, but he might want his own kind."

The priest sighed as he glanced at the boy. It was as if the word *polack* had been scrawled across his forehead. "What a neighborhood this is," he said quietly. "You would think that with everyone so poor, there'd be no room for hate."

He began to question the boy, who responded to the man's sympathetic voice. It was an old story the priest had heard many times of Irish kids ganging up on the non-Irish. He had to smile when Paulie hesitantly told him of the 1-4-All Club—*One for all against the Irish.*

"I know how you feel, Paul. I'm a Hell's Kitchen boy myself. But Mr. Duffy's a good man, and if I speak to him he'll give you part-time work. That is, if you can manage it."

"I will!" Paulie cried. "Thanks, Father."

The boy's eyes lit up, and although it was gray on the street, the two office windows rising tall and bleak (Father McGinley hadn't switched on the electricity), the priest felt as if the darkening office had been transformed into an altar.

"Don't thank me, Paul," Father McGinley said gently. "This terrible neighborhood! And yet there is good here. You know the old Hell's Kitchen saying, If a man has three sons one will become a cop, the second a gangster, the third a priest. My brother is a cop out in Queens but there were only two of us," he smiled. "I'll talk to Mr. Duffy, Paul. Come see me in a few days."

"I will, an' thank you, Father."

Paulie almost stumbled as he left the office. What a guy, he thought.

He felt his own unworthiness and then, as the wind from the river almost blew the cap from his head, the wide crosstown street lifted into sight, sharp and startling. People were hurrying home from work, trollies jangled by, and again he was surrounded by the sights and sounds of the world that had been his from childhood.

He cut down his own block, passing the shoemaker's shop. Behind the plate-glass window, Angie was working with his old man, the two canary cages suspended over their heads. And although Mary must be in the kitchen cooking supper, he glimpsed her anyway, formed out of the night and the wind, out of the white electric bulbs shining in the shop. He rapped at the window, shouting so he could be heard: "Hey, Angie! Say hello to Mary, will yuh . . ."

Nights saw Georgie prowling Ninth Avenue with one single thing on his mind: tips for the Spotter and the Spotter's stickup boys.

With Christmas close, the first peacetime Christmas, Germany beaten and Kaiser Bill chopping wood in Holland, the stores kept late hours. On Ninth the packed snow had been crunched under countless boots and galoshes into a blackish mush; the curbs lined with spruces and firs of all sizes. Fragrant and odorous, a green wind of memory carried the forests of the old country into the hearts and minds of the steerage immigrants.

Cap pulled over his eyes, Georgie might have been another shopper—but the bargain he sought so tirelessly was money! What did these storekeepers do with their cash receipts? Were there many storekeepers like the cheese-store guy, who filled a bag with big bills to bring home to wifey? After three or four days and nights of steady work he found them: Massalini the fruit and vegetable store and Viereck the pork butcher. When Massalini closed up for the night he would fill a cloth bag with produce to take home; Viereck left his place with a bundle of meat. Georgie was pretty sure that there was a little green stuff stuck away inside. In order to be dead certain he played hookey from school, hanging around Massalini's all morning. At ten o'clock Massalini walked out of his store to Eighth Avenue and Georgie, his shadow, watched him enter the Franklin Savings Bank on the corner of Forty-second Street.

He reported to the Spotter. "Massalini's a guy like the cheese-store jewboy. Viereck, too, but I'm not a hundred percent sure about him."

"Okeh," said the Spotter. "We'll find out."

To Dutch, a gleeful Georgie said, "I called his fuckin' bluff. We're good as in!"

Ever since the Wortsman stickup Dutch had felt itchy, praying for the day when he could quit his job. Wortsman had never suspected him, and that made it worse. The boss's jokes no longer seemed funny; the slices of cheese Dutch munched on the sly tasteless as sawdust. "All I can think of," he kept confessing to Georgie, "is gettin' out an' movin' into a lil ol' room of our own." He'd begun to feel cramped living at home, the whole family crowded in the kitchen these winter nights, a pot of coffee bubbling on the coal stove, the old man reading his newspaper and yapping away in German every once in a while how the war had been lost because of traitors in Berlin, his sister Gertie playing on the floor with her dolls, always underfoot like a cockroach, his brother Emil no better with his marbles. And when he went to bed it was Emil sharing it with him, kicking and tossing and hogging the blankets.

"Yuh know, Georgie," Dutch would say plaintively. "I'm only afraid somethin' or other's goin' to jinx us."

Georgie laughed. What was going to jinx them? A busted mirror, a black cat, a hunchback? Dutch had to laugh, too. He couldn't explain what'd turned him superstitious. He had stopped dropping in on Paulie of an evening when there was nothing better to do. It was too creepy what with Paulie's old lady, her face white as flour and sitting so quiet in her rocker near the coal stove. And Paulie? There was a changed guy.

"I dunno but we got nothin' much to talk about," he complained to Georgie.

"Hell, Dutch, you're not fair. The guy's just dead beat. Painting part-time for old Duff like being a janitor wasn't enough."

"Yeh, that's it!" Dutch exclaimed. "That harp Duffy!"

That night they were on their way to Milligan's Pool Parlor, their coat collars pulled up over their ears against the wind.

"That mick priest McGinley over at Holy Cross got Paulie the job," Georgie said. "Paulie told me all about it when we were eating lunch. That Paulie could be a priest himself! Hey, Dutch, can you see Paulie in a turnaround collar all dressed in black!" he laughed. "Paulie was always a prize dope, smart as he is. Hell, I'd like to see a priest praying over the Spotter before they dumped him into the grave. Him and his damn probation! There's a bastard I'm going to get even with someday!"

Dutch pulled his coat collar higher around his neck. It wasn't the wind that'd sent a shiver down his back. It was Georgie.

FOURTEEN

THE mirror above the kitchen sink centered Paulie's anxious face as he combed and parted his hair straight down the middle. A new style he'd copied out of a magazine advertisement for Arrow shirts.

From the table where she had been doing her homework Ava peeked at her big brother, a smile spreading across her lips like a smear of raspberry jam. "Paulie, Paulie," she singsonged. "I know somebody in love with somebody—"

She lowered her head when her mother scolded her and flipped a page in her school book, pretending to be engrossed in her reading. All was quiet for a few seconds. Then Ava began to giggle as if she had the Sunday funnies before her. Little Christina burst into laughter and danced her doll across the table's checkered oilcloth.

Mrs. Bolkonski in her rocker near the pink-lidded stove had to smile. Paulie snapped his fingers at his giggling sisters, and as his mother resumed sewing the doll dress on her lap, he thought she looked pretty good. Almost as good as in the days before she'd gotten sick.

Through the white gas mantle a golden light enveloped her lowered head. She never complained, he thought, cooking supper as always, making his lunch for school. When Ava and Christina got ready for bed she would tell them the stories he himself had heard as a child. Stories of the giant with eyes of ice and the witches who only left the dark forest to steal little babies.

One evening Cuomo the shoemaker on leaving the flat had whispered to Paulie, "Your mother she like-a da Madonna. . . ."

He would never forget that remark—or forget what she had to say about his talk with Father McGinley:

"He is a good priest. A good priest loves all men and loves God most of all." Stroking his young strong hand, she had murmured: "I have heard you cursing the Irish when you used to play in the backyard."

"Yes, mama," he had admitted. "I still hate 'em."

"Do you hate Father McGinley and Mr. Duffy, too?"

"They're dif'rent."

She had kissed his cheek and said, "You are a good son but there is a wild spirit in you as there was in your father."

She had said no more, but he'd known what she meant. His father was a drinker, quick with his fists, and with the liquor in him always ready for a fight.

He reknotted his necktie and walked from the mirror to kiss his mother and sisters good night. "When mama goes to bed," he said. "You girls clean up the kitchen. Tomorrer's Sunday, don't forget." Buttoning his mackinaw, he unlocked the door and hurried down the hallway to the street.

A cold wind like some waiting tough nipped at his ears. He lashed out with his trusty right, shadowboxing down the sidewalk. Another right! A left on the button!

One by one he K.O.d a mob of enemies including the biggest and most dangerous of the lot. West, beyond the last avenue, the faint whistle of a passing tug warned him to keep up his guard, and with a swift uppercut he smashed the prize sneak who wouldn't stay down. He cursed that old blood disease.

An El roared by on Ninth in a flash of yellow windows. He crossed the gutter to the shoe repair shop. The window was dark, the machines still. Cloth hoods covered the cages of the two canaries. He pressed the button.

Mr. Cuomo opened the door, and in a low voice asked Paulie about his mother.

"She's feelin' a little better," he said, following the stoop-shouldered shoemaker to the partitioning curtain that divided the front from the rear. He blinked at the light in the kitchen.

"Hello, Paulie," he heard Mary say, and only then did he become aware of Angie sitting near his sister.

" 'Lo," he muttered and slumped into a chair.

The shoemaker had walked into his bedroom, to return in a gray coat, a black floppy hat on his head. He explained that he was leaving the house to see his friend Da Costa the florist.

When he was gone, Angie snorted. "He can go drinkin' wine but no movin' pitchers for us."

"Don't be mad," Mary pleaded.

"Don't be mad!" Angie mimicked. "Kids, that's what we are to him, the big boss! Maybe you're a kid, Mary, but I woik all day same as him."

"We can play casino, Angie—"

"Yuh can play! I'm beatin' it—"

"Where you going, Angie?" Mary asked.

"Nowhere! Where can I go? Got no friends 'cept Paulie!" Glowering he raised one foot, "An' a whole pack-a busted shoes. 'Hey, Angie didja put them heels on?' " he mimicked a customer. " 'Hey, Angie, I want real leather soles, none-a this cardboard.' " He grabbed his cap hanging on a wall hook, and almost running, he shot through the partitioning curtain, slamming the street door behind him.

"Angie had an argument with papa," Mary said.

"Yeh?"

"We can play casino," he heard her saying calmly, as if this wasn't the first time that they'd been alone in the house. He'd expected her to get the cards, but instead she began to talk. He was too excited to really listen, mumbling yesses and noes to her questions. His mother was feeling better, yeh. Mary smiled and said it must be Christmas, and what was he giving Ava and Christina? He shrugged his shoulders.

"Paulie, I guess you haven't much money for presents," she was saying.

Her voice was soft, but he stiffened in his chair resentfully as if she'd slapped him, not with her hand but with some hard leather glove she had borrowed.

"Aw," he muttered at the whiplash of poverty, "don't yuh worry! I'll get some money."

She sighed, "Don't be mad, Paulie, but I got some money saved, seven dollars almost. I could loan it to you."

Tears filled his eyes and he wiped them, his hostility a

wetness that he got rid of when he wiped his fingers on his pants.

"Poor Paulie," she said.

He stared at her, muttering that he didn't want her pity. He could've kicked himself when he saw her lips quivering. "Mary, how's school?" he blurted, not knowing what else to say.

"School?" she said and laughed. "There's no school until Monday, Paulie."

She left the table and got a deck of cards. Mary shuffled the cards; Paulie picked up the four she dealt him: a ten of clubs, a six of spades, a king of diamonds, a queen of clubs. He studied them and instantly forgot what they were, glancing at the four cards, faces up, between them.

"You play, Paulie. I'm the dealer."

He stared at the cards on the table and matched them with the four in his trembling fingers. Clubs, spades, diamonds streaked across his mind. "I can't play," he said, casting his cards down.

In the silent kitchen the only sound was the ticking of the clock on the wall: a long coffin-shaped clock with a gilt pendulum swinging behind the glass cover. "Mary," he began, and frightened at his own courage he reached out his arm. When she clasped his hand he smiled and smiled, as if he would never wear any other expression on his face, not if he lived to be an old man. "Mary," he said again, and rising up from his chair, still holding her hand, he went toward her.

She stood up, and as he approached, raised her head as if she'd stepped out of the silver screens on Eighth Avenue.

It was their first kiss.

116

FIFTEEN

Iᴛ was a thrill to be one of the boys at a beer party in the back room of Cleary's saloon on Eleventh Avenue. No fancy dive this one, like Quinn's on Eighth, and if Dutch felt right at home in the Badger hangout, leave it to Georgie to bellyache.

"What a dump," he'd whispered in Dutch's ear, not that anyone could hear him, the noise so thick you could almost slice it and put it in a box.

Anyone with the price was welcome up front—bums from the neighborhood, hoboes off the Weehawken Ferry. But to Dutch, filling his glass out of the squat wooden keg on the table, the beer party was like another graduation with the Spotter himself handing out the diplomas.

"I want you to meet Dutch Yaeger and Georgie Alston," the Spotter had said, and for a couple of minutes the limelight was on the new gang members, their hands shaken, their backs slapped with Bughead Moore crushing Dutch's fingers in a mitt big as a ham. The Bughead, weighing two hundred pounds, also nicknamed the Man Mountain, had introduced Dutch and Georgie to Ted Griffin, an ex-pug, and sprinkled their heads with beer.

"Yuh gotta be baptize'!" he'd howled drunkenly.

Just the same, it was a thrill to be one of the boys, to laugh at Red McMann's stories with the Bughead shouting, "Bullshit, lissen to some-a these guys yuh'd think yuh was hearin' somethin'!"

"Here's mud in yer eye!" cried Cockeye Smith, who was trusted by nobody, as Sarge Killigan, trusted by everybody, had already warned the new recruits.

Nearly all micks, Georgie was thinking, all smiles as he mentally glued one name after another to the faces that came and went in the blue cigarette smoke. There was Lefty Muldoon with the squinty eyes and Mike Riley who sported a white silk handkerchief in his jacket pocket and Georgie Connelly who kept blowing on a police whistle until he was stopped. But there was also Billy Muhlen, who looked as German as a plate of knockwurst; and Joey Kasow, a jewboy who believe it or not looked as Irish as corned beef and cabbage.

The Spotter hadn't stayed long. He'd blown in with Clip Haley, the Badger leader, tilted his derby back from his bony forehead, and wetted his whistle on a glass of beer. Then the pair were gone.

"Fuck 'em!" the Bughead yelled, and in the laughter Sarge Killigan sidled over to Georgie, whispering hoarsely, "Yuh can see the bastid's off his rocker. Keep clear o' him, Georgie."

"He doesn't worry me," Georgie smiled. With three or four beers inside of him, the little wheels spinning in his head had slowed down. Had the Spotter cheated him and Dutch on the Massalini and Viereck jobs? He had no notion what those stickups had netted, or for that matter how much dough there'd been in Wortsman's take-home bag. The cheese store had put twenty bucks in his pocket, into Dutch's, too, and although he'd done all the work on Massalini and Viereck with the Spotter handing him sixty bucks to split or not split, he had told Dutch: "The bastard wants us to have hard feelings. Even-steven, Dutch!" And he'd handed over three ten-dollar bills and cursed the Spotter for a prize cheat. "The bastard said that since we're in the gang we had to think of guys who need a little dough. Christ, if I had a dime for every buck he and Clip're holding out on! Aw, hell, the main thing's we're in. But we can't move yet, Dutch. With Massalini and Viereck and Wortsman the bulls got three stickups on Ninth to figure out. You'll have to keep working, and I'll have to keep going to that dumb high school. Maybe after New Year we can quit and get a room of our own. . . ."

The Spotter had his reasons, good and bad, for sending Georgie out stealing the department stores. Georgie's big brown eyes and girlish mouth that seemed as if it only opened to sing the praises of God the Father was the spitting image of a choirboy. A perfect getup to fool the department-store dicks. Yet that same baby face rubbed the Spotter like itching powder. Behind those big brown eyes there was a foxy grandpa. Only sixteen years old, the punk, the Spotter brooded, remembering how dumb he'd been at that age. He wasn't surprised when the little limey bastard squawked that shoplifting was kid's stuff.

The Spotter bawled him out. The first thing he had to learn was to take orders, and if he was told to go out and steal a lollipop out of a baby's mouth, that was what he had to do and no back talk. Georgie, as the Spotter had expected, crawled into his hole. Innocent as a baby he looked, which only confirmed the Spotter's doubts.

"I'm ready for anything you want me to do," Georgie said.

The very next day Georgie received his first lessons from Millie O'Toole, one of the Badger girls; the classroom was her furnished room south of the Pennsylvania tracks. She was older than Georgie by two years, half a head taller and on the heavy side, broad-hipped in a black skirt, her breasts inside her white blouse so full and round they seemed like packed snowballs.

"Always look sweet as milk," she said earnestly.

"That's easy for me," he smiled.

"Yeh," she laughed.

He got up and crossed to where she was leaning against the dresser, circling her waist with his arm. She pushed him off, her dark blue eyes incredulous; open-mouthed with an innocence that had once been hers.

"Did you see a ghost, Millie?"

"Lissen, yuh! Doncha get any idears or Clip'll nail yuh!"

"So you're Clip's girl? Why doesn't anybody tell me things?"

"I'm tellin' yuh an' don't yuh forget it!"

"You're just so pretty a feller gets ideas."

She had to smile at his nerve. Fresh as they came, she thought, studying his small neat face, still beardless, not even a bit of fuzz on his chin, and only a few hairs like faint pencil marks on his lip.

"A feller tells a girl she's pretty and he can get himself arrested. You are pretty, Millie."

Her contemptuous shrug proved to him that she hadn't swallowed the bait. She knew she wasn't pretty, he thought. Her nose was too small for her big mick face. But for kicks Georgie tried once again: "You're pretty in your own way, baby."

"Dat's enough, squirt! The Spotter tipped me off about yuh—"

"That's the Spotter all right. All tips."

"Doncha ever talk straight?" she asked him, genuinely puzzled.

His head tilted back on his slender neck as he laughed. He slapped his side and assured Millie he was the straightest guy she'd ever met in a month of Sundays. He glanced about the room, the unmade bed, the imitation oak dresser that looked as if its next destination was a junkyard, the girl leaning against it—a juicy piece, he was thinking.

There must have been something in his narrowed eyes, a catlike gleam maybe, that bothered the girl, for all her knowledge of men. If he'd been older, hard or mean in his looks, she wouldn't have been puzzled. But he was so young —Babyface the Spotter had named him—and because she was confused she latched on to what was sure and definite. Shoplifting. In the store, she said, you had to keep an eye peeled for the store dicks, thick as flies at Christmas. The best bet was to stick close to some woman shopping like he was one of the family. "Yuh gotta woik fast," she said and demonstrated, her hand darting at the dresser and in a second a bottle of perfume near the edge had vanished inside her skirt pocket. "A quick swipe, get it, an' only stuff that fits easy in yer mitt. Awright, le's see yuh try." And with the dresser as a make-believe counter she had him practicing for a solid hour.

On a winter morning with the red-jacketed Santas ringing bells on Thirty-fourth Street, a light snow white as their beards falling and specking the shoulders of the passersby, Millie and Georgie walked into R. H. Macy's.

"Remembuh," she said, "yer on yer own."

Shoppers crammed the aisles, two and three deep at the counters. A thousand hands, gloved and ungloved, fingered the merchandise; neckties bright as pennants, ladies wear, jewelry, porcelains. The clerks inserted the bills received from their customers and the sales slips for purchases into metal tubes. The tubes whizzed up from the counters toward the ceiling like miniature travel capsules, speeding overhead on the slenderest of tracks: the wires that connected every section to the cashiers on the mezzanine above the floor.

Georgie, following instructions, had lagged behind Millie. She was ahead of him now. He was on his own, he thought licking his dry lips. It's nothing, he told himself, anything dumb Millie can do, I can do. Her broad-brimmed hat with a huge bunch of wax grapes pinned to the band was no longer visible, swallowed up in a press of bobbing heads. His eyes shifted right and left, but he saw no store dicks; or maybe they were everywhere, for all he knew. You're getting cold feet, he taunted himself, and crossing to a counter of men's shirts he asked the clerk where the perfume was sold. He zigzagged through the Christmas crowd and behind a moving fence of faces stared at a counter that seemed like a row of glittering glass boxes. The perfume section! Just where a store dick'd be on the watch! Be careful, he warned himself. That fat guy in the derby? Nope, he's buying!

He appraised the customers and joined a lady in a mink coat and ostrich-feathered hat at one of the perfume counters. The clerk squeezed the bulb of a tiny bottle and the lady sniffed. Georgie forced a smile to his lips. If there were any dicks nearby he wanted them to think he was with the lady, one of the family. An intoxicating winter garden of flowers floated into his nostrils.

"How much is it?" the lady asked.

Georgie glanced at the bottles on the counter, some slender as hourglasses, others round and glossy and no bigger than the plums he'd swiped on 1-4-All raids over at Paddy's Market. The interiors of the bottles held all the colors of the rainbow, yellow and green, amber brown, and rosy pink. And as the clerk answered the questions of the ostrich-feathered lady, he peered at his own hand as if it were a stranger's. Detached from his body it seemed, the fingers closing on a crystalline bottle, square in shape like an oversized dice. And then the hand was gone and he realized he had the bottle of perfume safe inside his overcoat pocket.

That fat guy in the derby? Nope, he just can't make up his mind what to buy, Georgie thought, breathing deeply as if still another hand that'd been at his throat had released its grip.

The ostrich-feathered lady had opened her purse, unclipping a ten-dollar bill while he waited patiently—her darling son, he thought, with a bravado that by the second filled him with triumph—watching the clerk place the ten-dollar bill and sales slip inside a metal tube.

When the tube with its change shot back to the counter, transaction completed, the lady departed. He too left, walking so close to her their shoulders touched. Outside on the sidewalk in the falling snow a Salvation Army band seemed to be performing for him, their horns, drums, and cymbals celebrating not only the Prince of Peace but Georgie Alston, the champion shoplifter.

Christmas had come in cold, but the thermometer would sink even lower with the new year of 1919. In January and February the water in the tenement pipes froze and cracked the metal; every plumber boss could name his own price. Work around the clock for plumbers in Hell's Kitchen. Work, too, for the Badgers, night work. A plumber alone in a cellar was the easiest of marks. Peanut stuff in Clip Haley's opinion with the Spotter reminding the Badger leader that beggars couldn't be choosers, not with thirty guys in the gang. A buck here and a buck there was nothing to sneeze at.

"That's just your trouble," Clip said. "Yuh think only in bucks, yuh think small."

And again the number-two man in the gang swallowed the insult like a mint candy dusted with sugar. Clip ran the floating crap games, but it was pulling teeth to squeeze a twenty-dollar bill out of him to spread among the boys. *Me first* was his motto, and the whole gang knew it. Clip was always in a new suit and black patent-leather shoes a tap dancer might have worn, a ruby in his necktie; a show-off. With plenty of money to spend on fancy women but so cheap his own girl, Millie, had to go out shoplifting to make herself an honest dollar. Sooner or later, the Spotter consoled himself, he'd be taking over the leadership. For where did a hog, even the biggest and the fattest hog, end up but in the slaughterhouse.

A few days after the beer party they lunched together in an Italian restaurant. Clip, growling between forkfuls of spaghetti, complained that the Spotter must think he was a bank. "All these kids? Wot the hell do we need 'em for? This dutchie 'n' that limey punk?"

"You forget the limey did good with Massalini and Viereck—"

"Yeh, but wot I'm gettin' at is this. We got enough guys 'n' half of them's free-loaders."

"We'll be needin' 'em when this Prohibition—"

"That Quinn don't know his ass from his elbow! This country'll never go dry! This country's a free country!" Clip said with the fervor of a true patriot. It'll never let a bunch-a lousy drys close up the saloons!"

The Spotter didn't waste his breath arguing. All he said was that it was a funny time. Did the country want to go to war to save the limies? It didn't, but that bluenose Wilson, who by rights should've been a minister like his old man, had other ideas.

"That's all ole stuff!" Clip retorted as if the war had happened a hundred years ago. "I don't want no more guys in the Badgers. Get me? We got enough. What they're gonna do I dunno. Okeh, the limey's earned his keep, but wot about that pignosed dutchie?"

"He'll earn his keep with the plumbers. . . ."

The Spotter, like a superintendent in a factory picking the right man for the right job, didn't waste a minute wondering how Dutch could fit in. A strongarm if there ever was one. Over a beer in the backroom of Cleary's saloon he had a talk with Red McMann. "I want you to show'm the ropes, Red."

The next night the two Badgers met on the corner of Forty-third and Ninth, the sidewalks empty except for a solitary drunk wobbling homeward, the stars white and bright as if chipped out of icicles.

"Yuh ain't nervous, Dutch?" Red asked. "Like I told yuh, there's nothin' to it."

And there was nothing to it. The Spotter's boys had been keeping an eye on a half dozen plumber shops. "See where they go to work at night," the Spotter had ordered.

Red McMann and Dutch crossed under the El tracks, hurried down a side street, their breath flowing like steam.

"Here we are," said Red, leading the way into a tenement. In the vestibule's dim yellow light—a high-class house this one, with electricity—his nighttime face emerged in profile as if cut out of the same metal as the gleaming letter boxes. The inside door was locked.

"Locked, ain't it?" Dutch whispered nervously.

The redhead turned, his eyes shadowed by the peak of his cap. "Don't piss in your pants, kid," he grinned. "Save that for when the goin's rough."

He pulled off his gloves, fished a skeleton key out of his pocket, inserted it in the lock, turning it as delicately as if it were made out of silk. Smiling, he pushed open the door. In that sardine box of a vestibule with its glowing electric bulb something like electricity quickened Dutch's heart. They moved fast down the hallway.

Red whispered. "I'll back yuh up, Dutch. Yuh got it straight?"

Dutch nodded and yanked a blackjack out of his mackinaw pocket, to be told to take his gloves off. "Yuh need a solid grip, kiddo." Dutch gulped, shoved the blackjack into his pocket, removed his leather gloves, rammed them into his second pocket. Neither of them had paused, advancing on the cellar at the far end of the hallway. Dutch felt as if he were running between high walls, taller than the El pillars, breathing hoarsely like a winded sprinter. The cellar door wasn't quite closed. A vertical bar of yellow light wiggled in his sight like some finishing line. Jeez, he prayed, don't let me monk up.

His fingers tightened on the taped blackjack as Red swung the cellar door wide open, the bar of yellow light no longer a thin line, a yellow wall from which Red's voice echoed like a pistol shot: "Hey, plumb-err. Land-lordd wants yuh to hurr-ry overr to Forty-fifth. Four eighteen Forty-fifth. An e-mergency-y there . . ."

Another voice sounded out of the cellar, out of a bottom deeper than any pit: "Who're you?"

Down the wooden stairs Dutch rushed toward the up-tilted face of the plumber, pale and waxy in the light of the single bulb dangling from a wire in the ceiling. "Land-lordd, that's who! Gen'rall Poish-ingg, that's who!" he heard Red saying behind him from the top of the flight. He couldn't see Red. But for a second the eyes of the plumber might have been his own, and without turning his head, he *saw* Red McMann. Red, gun in hand, everything clicking according to plan. Gun, blackjack, plumber.

"Stick your hand ups." Red was saying.

The wooden stairs creaked under Dutch's weight. It was a short flight, but with his heart pounding it seemed to lengthen before his eyes, endless, like the snow-covered steps of the General Post Office on Eighth Avenue where in another winter the 1-4-Alls had climbed, dragging their sleds to the top before shooting down again to the icy sidewalk. Dutch blinked and the memory was gone.

On the cellar floor, sections of pipe, couplings and elbows, wrenches and pliers formed a semicircle around the plumber's open toolbag. Fear had glazed the eyes of the cornered man, pulled his lips apart, shriveled the muscles in his back and shoulders as if he just had strength enough to keep his arms high above his head.

"Nobody's gonna hurt yuh!" Red was saying. "Stick them tools back inna bag!"

Dutch, his blackjack ready, not a foot away from the plumber, watched him obey the order.

"Now your wallet!" Red said. "Toss it onna bag!"

Like an oversized black card, the wallet missed the bag.

"Bum throw," Red said. "Turn round, yuh! An' keep them hands up! Okeh," he said to Dutch.

It was the signal they had rehearsed. So easy to rehearse, so hard to do. Dutch hesitated.

"Okeh!" Red repeated.

Biting on his lower lip Dutch stepped forward and swung the blackjack. The plumber dropped as if a manhole had opened up under his feet. From the top of the flight Red's voice snapped like a horsewhip. "Le's go!" Dutch winced, staring at the crumpled heap on the cellar floor, so silent now. The poor bastard, he was thinking.

"Goddammit, le's go!"

Dutch picked up the wallet, picked up the toolbag. The sixty or seventy pounds it weighed seemed no heavier than a couple of greasy rags lying on the floor.

"You're okeh," Red said out on the street.

And *okeh* was the word that circulated through the gang. Dutch was *okeh* with Red, *okeh* with the Spotter.

"Next time," said the Spotter, squeezing Dutch's biceps. 'Next time just a li'l tap. You sent that plumber to the hospital, and the one thing the cops don't like is homicide."

Dutch was silent. What was there to say? That he didn't want to hurt the plumber or use the blackjack even, the guy wasn't putting up a fight—swinging out only because Red ordered it and he was too scared to go against Red or the Spotter.

All through January, Millie and Georgie hit the big department stores on Herald Square; Macy's one day, Gimbel's or Saks' the next. The well-dressed shoppers still celebrating the end of the war, spending money like drunken sailors (as Millie never tired of saying) started Georgie thinking. Shoplifting was a piker's game with nothing much to show for it after the fence took his cut.

Lift a purse and you had the real McCoy, money in the hand, and no fence grabbing off the lion's share.

Without saying a word to Millie or even to Dutch, all on his lonesome, he entered Gimbel's, the main floor his hunting ground, his eyes on the alert for a rich dame. He settled finally on a woman in a fur coat that reached to her ankles. As he would tell Dutch afterward, the smell of money was plastered all over her. The woman had finished shopping, her purchases under one furry arm, and in the other an alligator handbag whose glossy brown rippled leather seemed stamped with dollar signs. As she slowly made her way through the dense crowds toward the exit, Georgie followed. He unbuttoned his mackinaw, ready for action. You needed a place to hide a lifted purse— Georgie had figured the whole thing out, A to Z.

Now! he thought at the exit. Sidestepping around two women with arms loaded with purchases he rushed forward and snatched the alligator handbag, shoving it inside his coat as he ran into the street. He heard the lady shouting, "Stop him! Stop him! He stole my . . ." but he was already a dozen yards away, losing himself in the slow-moving procession outside the shining plate-glass windows, no longer running, not even turning his head, an innocent pedestrian. He stepped into the first side-entrance he passed, back on the main floor again. He'd rehearsed this, too, in his bedroom. No purse snatcher would return to the scene of his crime—wasn't that how a dumb store dick might think?

Nice and steady . . . the phrase echoed like a jingle in his head as he stepped out to the street again, into the cold blue afternoon. Nice and steady . . . He glanced at his reflection in the department-store windows, smiling at the whole big wide world: a world of the blind. No one could see that handbag. No one! The thought delighted him.

I did it! he exulted. Funny that dame hollering. A rich dame from her looks. Wonder how much dough? Fifty bucks? A hundred? A thousand? Crazy!

The store windows on Thirty-fourth, lit up in the darkening afternoon with night hanging impalpable in the freezing air, seemed to shine just for him. The travelers headed for Pennsylvania Station on Thirty-third, strangers though they were, all wished him well.

When he reached his own block, his own house, he sprinted up the stairs. Nice and steady . . . But he no longer felt so steady, the alligator bag under his coat burning with a flame that left no scar. Who the hell knew what was in it? Maybe nothing? Suppose that dame had spent all her dough? Suppose there was only a stinking handkerchief inside the bag? A stinking comb, nail file, powder puff?

He unlocked the door of his flat, blinking when he heard footsteps, his mother's voice.

"Is that you, Georgie?"

"Yeh," he answered and walked into the kitchen. The fading light of that winter afternoon mantled her shoulders; the linoleum-covered floor a shadowy sheet.

"Where have you been, Georgie?"

"With Paulie," he lied.

She shook her head and he could see she didn't believe him. "You never tell me any more where you go or what you do." Her mouth creased at the corners, as she scolded him. Her face was pale, his nipped red, which only accentuated their resemblance. Thin and slender, both of them, with the same black hair and large lustrous eyes.

"You worry too much about me." He smiled and blew her a kiss with his free hand as he went into his room, closing the door. She called to him: Why was he always locking himself in. "A feller wants his privacy," he replied, frowning now. A pain in the neck his mother was, always whining where did you go? why don't you do your homework? your report card's a disgrace.

He had intended to open the alligator handbag in his room, but suddenly fearful that she might be tailing him, he hurried through his parents' bedroom into the parlor. It was almost night but he didn't switch on the electricity. Dark as it was, he felt as if some bright, intense light was pouring through the curtained windows. The room seemed strange to him—the green plush sofa and green matching chairs, the beaded lamps, the plaster cast of Queen Victoria on its walnut stand. A regular undertaker's parlor, he'd often thought. Different now, a hideaway because of what he'd brought there. He ached to pull out the handbag, hesitated, ears pinned flat against his head, listening. He wanted to be dead sure his mother wouldn't be barging in.

The handbag was in his trembling hands as if shoved there by a ghostly pickpocket. He opened it, his chest heaving at what he saw: an address book, a powder puff, a silver comb and mirror. He ransacked the inner pockets and found a billfold, narrow and elegant and also made out of alligator hide: the bills neatly folded. "Christ!" he exclaimed. Wetting his thumb and forefinger he counted them one by one. "Sixty-four bucks!" he whispered.

Magical pieces of paper, for between one greenback and the next, that longed-for room of his own assumed shape and dimension.

Five minutes later, ignoring his mother's questions of where he was going, he left the flat after caching fifty dollars under the mattress in his room. The remainder, fourteen dollars, he had returned to the alligator handbag, which he carried inside his mackinaw, clutched under his left armpit. A little present for Millie, he thought, as he dashed down the stairs to the street. The lampposts stretched before him, beacons of light leading to her room. He passed the house where Paulie and Dutch lived—wait'll Dutch heard! he thought—the faded number, 355, on the glass pane above the door revolving like the numbers on a carnival wheel, the winner showing up: 64.

Sixty-four bucks, he calculated like an insane bookkeeper. Fifty bucks under the mattress! Fourteen in the alligator bag! Sixty-four bucks!

He crossed Thirty-fourth, and two blocks below entered a street of furnished roominghouses and little French table d'hôtes (the "frog block," as the Irish called Thirty-second), smiling when he came to Millie's house. He climbed three brownstone stairs, rang the bell in the vestibule above which her handlettered name *Mildred O'Toole* had been inserted. The lock clicked and he raced up the stairs, knocked at her door, breezed inside, and without a word held out the alligator handbag like a bouquet of flowers materialized in the hand of a stage magician.

"Wot's dat?" she said.

"A Christmas present for you, Millie."

"Christmas is over."

"Not for me."

"Where'd yuh get it?"

The rich dark brown leather with its gold-plated clasp was out of place in that room where every stick of furniture seemed off a secondhand truck; the dresser branded with the stubbed-out cigarettes of a nameless troupe of roomers; the rumpled bed sagging in the middle from the fly-by-nights who'd slept here for a week or two before vanishing.

"A nice lady at Gimbel's gave it to me, Millie."

Her eyes lifted from the bag in his small white hand to his grinning face. "Yuh snatched it, huh? Yuh shouldn'!"

"Open it up, Millie."

She unsnapped the clasp, stared at the bills he had placed on top of the address book, powder puff, and silver comb. Her mouth, unsnapped, too, her red lips parted like a child's.

He approached the girl, advised her to throw the junk away, slipping his arm around her waist. She pushed him off.

"There's fourteen bucks in that bag, Millie. It's all yours. So don't you think you ought to give me a kiss?"

"Georgie! Yuh must be drunk or crazy. Clip—"

"Clip don't have to know, baby," he said, grabbing her wrist.

She wrenched free, dodged his hand, "Yuh li'l rat!" she shouted and threw the handbag to the floor. "Take it an' beat it!" she cried. "Of all the no-good lousy rats—"

A buffoon's grin on his lips, Georgie sauntered over to

the bed, seated himself. "Cool off, Millie. Clip doesn't give one good damn about you—"

"Beat it, I said!"

"Do you ever see any of his dough?"

"Nobody's askin' yuh—"

"I'll beat it in a minute," he promised. "But you got to listen to me. He lets you hustle the stores while he spends his dough on any sweet-talking dame that comes along."

"Shut up, yuh bastid!"

"The truth hurts—"

"Beat it, yuh limey bastid!"

"That's no way to talk to me!" And before she could fend him off, he rushed forward, his head lowered, diving under her wildly swinging arms. She squirmed out of his grip and back he flew from her flattened palms on his chest; the dresser mirror reflecting his passage.

"I'll tell Clip—"

"Tell'm this!" he said, bouncing toward her like a rubber ball. Seizing her blouse, he ripped it down the middle.

Speechless, she tried to pull the torn edges together over her slip.

"Clip treats you like dirt. Get wise!" he jeered.

"He'll kill yuh for dis!" she screamed.

Georgie stooped, picked up the alligator handbag. "I'll tell Clip you snatched it and wanted to keep it and keep the money! I'll tell'm you were holding out—"

"Who's gonna believe a sneaky bastid like yuh?"

"Maybe yes, maybe no. He won't know what to believe. I said I was going and I am. I'll find Clip and give him the bag and the dough."

"Jesus Christ," she wailed. "Yuh try dat an' I'll kill yuh myself, so help me Gawd!"

"Clip won't know what to believe. Who knows, maybe you held out on him before I caught you in the act?"

Fiery red her cheeks, her forehead, her neck; tears in her eyes who long ago had forgotten how to weep. Her shoulders drooped and the tears flowed down her powdered cheeks.

He tossed the handbag on the dresser and walked over to the girl, his eyes gleaming. Going on seventeen was he, or seventy? "How about that kiss, baby?" he smiled.

Wiping her eyes she looked at him pathetically, "Yuh devil," she muttered.

SIXTEEN

WHO had thought of the idea to meet after school? Mary hated to think that it must be her, not Paulie. A boy should've been the one. Not a girl. It would've been less wrong, she felt.

At night she turned restlessly in her bed. A flimsy wooden partition separated the girl from her father and brother who slept in the larger part of what had once been a single bedroom. She could hear Angie muttering in his sleep, her father snoring. Sometimes she imagined the partition splitting down the center, her father's face appearing, grim and malicious, shaking his fist and shouting: *You're a bad girl Mary....* She must be bad, she thought miserably, who after that first kiss dreamed of a second kiss and a third.

One Saturday evening, after a three-handed game of casino—her father was visiting Da Costa the florist—she had walked Paulie to the street door. Dark as it was in the shop, nevertheless she could see Paulie as he had been in the bright kitchen, his blond hair falling straight as if each hair had been ironed, his eyes as light as her own were dark.

"Paulie," she'd said so quietly that even a mouse couldn't have heard her. "Maybe we can meet some day after school —go home together?" Trembling as she spoke, biting on her lips.

Paulie, in a voice as low as her own, whispered, "Your father—"

"My father's funny that way. He doesn't have to know. We could meet if you want, Paulie?" not believing it was her own voice talking; it was as if some other girl were putting the words in her mouth.

"When?" he was saying.

Her heart shook like a holiday noisemaker. "Maybe Wednesday," she said. "Yeh, Wednesday."

"At your school?"

"No, not there. The corner of Fourteenth and Ninth. That'd be best." She lifted her hand to his face, her fingers on his cheek annihilating all distance, quivering when they kissed. "Good night, Paulie."

"Wednesday, Mary?"

"Wednesday."

Once a week, all through February with the icicles permanent fixtures hanging from the store signs, and all through March blowing snow one day and warming gusts the next, they met at the corner of Fourteenth and Ninth. If it wasn't too raw a day they would walk northwards, their destination the El station on Twenty-third Street. Those nine blocks were like another country to which they'd escaped, a place where there were no watchdog fathers, no sick mothers, no schools, no homework, no floors for Paulie to scrub, no rooms to paint on one of Duffy's jobs. Another country where, even with snow underfoot, winter was forever banished. The shops they passed were no different from those in their own neighborhood, but even on gray days their plate-glass windows stretched endlessly like some enchanted wall enclosing the two of them.

They would climb the flight of stairs to the El station, the train thundering in. They would sit down in one of the double side seats, Mary next to the window, the El slicing through the tenements lining the tracks, watching the Els going by or perhaps a child holding a doll and instructing it, *Look at the big train. . . .*

At the Forty-second Street station they would linger in the waiting room, warm their hands at the fiery-red pot-bellied stove. And when the last of the passengers went down the stairs to the street, their lips would meet in a swift farewell kiss.

Georgie had given Millie the alligator handbag, but he sensed that in a queer sort of way he was still holding on to it, hidden in some secret pocket of the mind like a lucky rabbit's foot. With one rub sixty-four dollars had dropped into his lap and opened up Milly like an oyster.

All his, those sixty-four bucks and no depending on the Spotter for a crummy slice of the pie! Outsmarted that bastard, outsmarted Clip. And last but not least, the furnished room he'd set his heart on was no longer a pipedream.

"You can't quit your job yet," he told an impatient Dutch. "And I'll keep going to school until I figure out a clean break. We don't want our folks flying all over the coop."

After thinking it over, he decided that Paulie was just the

guy they wanted as a go-between. At Miles Cafeteria at lunch period he announced that this was his last day at De Witt Clinton. He could see that Paulie had brushed off his remark as if it were one of the pesky cafeteria flies.

"You think I'm just bellyaching?" Georgie smiled and pulled out a letter he'd written less than two hours ago in the school library. "Do me a favor, Paulie, and give this to my mother, okeh? It says that me and Dutch're hitting the road for California. Tell her that's the way it is and no use blowing her top."

Paulie had stopped eating. A slice of cold meat dropped from his homemade sandwich. "Yuh must be kiddin'—"

The California thing was baloney, Georgie admitted. He and Dutch'd rented a room on West Twenty-sixth down in Chelsea where nobody knew them from a hole in the ground. The California thing was a dodge. "If we're out there, they'll have to lump it, right?" he grinned. "After a while they'll quit worrying." Inspired by this consideration of his mother's feelings, he plucked a ten-dollar bill from his wallet. "This is for your old lady, Paulie. For medicine or something."

When Paulie refused it, Georgie laughed, "Okeh, be proud! How is your mother these days, Paulie?"

Mrs. Bolkonski had her ups and downs. One week Paulie had to hire a neighborhood woman at a dollar a day to take care of his mother while he was at school. Mrs. Olnik was Polish but that hadn't helped. His mother, sick as she was, wouldn't have another woman bossing her around. She would be forced to listen to a regular nurse; that was Dr. Reich's opinion. It was the white uniform, Dr. Reich had said, the authority. Dr. Reich knew a retired nurse who'd come in for four dollars a day. Five days a week would be enough, Mondays to Fridays, while Paulie was at school.

"That's twenty a week, Paulie," Georgie said. "Ain't that what you get as a janitor? How could you swing it? Didn't you tell me the other day Duffy canned you?"

"He didn't can me. He had to give his sister's kid the job I was doin'."

"Same thing!"

"Don't be such a wise guy!"

"How're you going to swing it, Paulie?"

"My uncle in Chicago promised to send five bucks a week, and Ginsberg the tailor on Thirty-ninth said if his delivery boy quit he'd give me his job."

"Nickel tips, maybe a dime?" Georgie scoffed.

"It's something."

"When would you do it? After school?"

"Yeh, like when I was workin' for Duffy. An' if worse comes to worse maybe I'll quit school."

And make what? Georgie wanted to know. "Hey!" he exclaimed. "What about that priest at Holy Cross? Will he help you out if your mother needs a regular nurse?"

"He said he'd help me as much as he could."

"What about a regular nurse?" Georgie persisted.

Paulie shook his head. "He said she might have to go to the hospital. The hell with that!" he burst out. "My mother's not goin' to no charity hospital. She's not gonna be no guinea pig for a bunch of internes to practice on!"

Georgie, eyeing the fierce face that had sprung up on the other side of the white-tiled table, felt a strange emotion. It was as if he were seeing his own face in a distorting mirror. A fighter, Paulie, just like me. He jabbed his fork into the last of his chocolate pie, smearing it like a dark brown paint over his plate. The sensation of *likeness* was gone as swiftly as it had come. The bastard was so good— and a hell of a lot of good it'd do him! He didn't have the chance of a snowball in hell, the dumb polack.

He glanced at Paulie with unconcealed contempt. Nickel tips his speed, handouts from uncles in Chicago and tight-fisted priests. "And you fell for that priest's gab?" he sneered.

"It wasn't gab!" Paulie said angrily. "He got me work with Duffy an' he said he'd talk to others!"

"They've got plenty dough if they want to hand it out—"

"What the hell do you know? They got a million poor—"

"That's their line—"

"Shut up! Yuh think yuh know everything, don't you?"

"I know more'n you, Paulie! I always have! But that got nothing to do with our being friends. We've always been friends, and I mean that. Now this letter to my mother— You'll back me and Dutch up, won't you, about California?"

"Sure, if you want me to do it."

"Thanks, Paulie. I've always liked you, and you know why? You've got real guts even though you're full of dumb ideas."

"Our ideas're dif'rent—"

"Where will yours get you?"

"I could ask yuh the same thing."

"Okeh, okeh! Be a nickel chaser, but if you ever need

some real dough, you go to Cleary's saloon on Eleventh. I'd give you the address of the furnished room, but me and Dutch might be moving if we don't like it. You'll remember? Cleary's on Eleventh. If I'm not there they'll know where I am. Just ask somebody in the back room."

"I don't get it."

"This is between us, Paulie. Swear honest to God you won't tell nobody."

"Honest to God," Paulie said.

"Cleary's the Badger hangout. Me and Dutch're Badgers."

"Jesus Christ!" Paulie exclaimed. "Yuh shouldn't—"

"Never mind that stuff!" And pulling out his wallet he again offered the tenner and again Paulie refused it. Georgie's neat handsome head was motionless for a second, his large lustrous eyes fixed on Paulie's face. "Take the bill, for Christ sake! If it'll make you feel better, make believe you got it from that priest of yours. Hey, I got another idea! You can ask Old Cheesehead for Dutch's job!"

When Paulie was with Mary all his problems drifted away like the swift runaway clouds that had come with April. Saturday nights, when Mary's father was drinking wine with Da Costa the florist, they were often alone. Angie would skip out. Even homely Angie had found a girl. Alone in the shoemaker's kitchen they would look at each other for a second. Love was a miracle impossible to believe.

"I love you, Mary," he would whisper, and when she echoed his I-love-you, the stern image of her father began to crumble into fragments.

With summer their meetings after school ended. He only

saw her Saturday nights when he was through working at the cheese store. Soon after his talk with Georgie he had seen Wortsman. So he was a friend of Henry Yaeger? And what did Henry want with California? Wortsman was pleased that Paulie attended high school, advising him to stay there. Nothing like an education, the storekeeper declared. He'd hired Paulie for Saturdays, paying a dollar and a half, and promising him a job when school let out. He had kept his promise, and maybe because Paulie was a high school boy, he paid him nine dollars a week. Three more than he'd paid Paulie's friend Henry Yaeger.

"I got two jobs again, Mary," Paulie had said ruefully. "Trouble is, I never see you much."

With the first chill autumn days his mother had sickened. "I am like the leaves the wind will take," she said. Paulie left like a leaf himself, blown away from all secure holds. In October the retired nurse Dr. Reich knew began coming to the house five days a week. But how long would the money he'd saved working for Wortsman and Duffy last? Even with the five-dollar money order that arrived each week from Chicago?

SEVENTEEN

"**I** smell money," the Spotter said when Prohibition closed down the saloons in January 1920.

"Wot's America comin' to anyway?" Clip mourned.

But Clip, as the Spotter had often observed (in strict confidence, Spotter to Spotter speaking), was solid ivory between the ears. "The hell with America," the Spotter retorted. "Quinn's got some ideas that'll do us all some good."

More than ideas. The saloonkeeper had sniffed the wind of change carrying the rich ripe smell of big money. He was prepared to go illegal, and the gang figured large in his plans. All through the year 1919 when times were tough for the Badgers he would peel off a century note to hand to the Spotter. "That'll buy some groceries for the boys," he would say in his thick brogue.

The Badgers had been scratching along, stealing whatever wasn't nailed down, knocking over plumbers in the winter and not too proud winter or summer to send one of the gang's girls out on the street.

In the first wild days of Prohibition, with every second cop shutting an eye if he was taken care of, the Spotter and

Clip, backed by Quinn, opened their first oasis for the thirsty.

"Speakeasies" they would soon be called: a new language was in the making. Men like Quinn would become known as "bootleggers," gangsters as "mobsters," gang leaders like the Spotter, newly risen out of the gutters of obscurity, glorified as "big shots."

By March, three months into the new year, the Badgers were operating nine speakeasies, selling whiskey Quinn purchased from saloonkeepers who'd closed their doors, as well as the gin and rye manufactured to meet the demand. Five hundred bucks bought a still that could make a hundred gallons a day. A shot of bootleg whiskey fetched two bits—a bargain—in the hole-in-the-wall speaks off the river; four bits once you walked under the El on Ninth Avenue; a buck a shot the closer you got to Broadway, once known as the Great White Way and now newly christened the Great Wet Way.

"Every Tom, Dick, an' Harry'll be rakin' in the dough," the ex-saloonkeeper declared, "but the lion's share'll go to the boys with the connections. Braggin's not me line but connections I got. All we want," said Quinn, "is our share o' the Kitchen."

It was one big Hell's Kitchen, stretching west from Eighth Avenue to the river, south to Chelsea below the Pennsylvania railroad tracks on Thirty-third Street, running north into the Fifties. The avenues east of Eighth Avenue were forbidden territory for the likes of Quinn, a fact he accepted philosophically. "The real money always winds up in the pockets of the big boys. A Larry Fay or a Waxey Gordon or an Ownie Madden."

The Spotter felt that he couldn't have found a better partner in a month of Sundays. The Spotter wasn't superstitious. A black cat to him was just another mouser and no imp of the devil. But when he moved out of his furnished room into that classy Hotel Berkeley on West Forty-sixth off Broadway, he couldn't help thinking, somebody up there must like me.

In his room the Spotter lay sleeplessly at night. Someone had to use the old bean, figure the flow of booze into the speaks on Thirty-ninth, Forty-first, Forty-fifth, Forty-seventh, Forty-eighth. Rye, gin, beer, a little bourbon but not too much—the West Side was a rye-drinking town—supply and demand but not too much supply. For if there was a raid, and the bottles got smashed, the loss could be held down. Then there was the weekly payroll, three guys to a speak—a bartender, a waiter, and a bouncer. There were also the roughhouse boys to smash up any guy "muscling" in—another new word—on Badger territory.

He and Quinn were a good team. The ex-saloonkeeper took care of the cops and the politicians, and although Christmas had come and gone, he kept giving away what he called "li'l Christmas presents." A good team—and it could've been a better one without Clip Haley. Okeh with fists but nothing beween the ears. Not that Quinn ever said that the Badger leader had to go. He didn't have to. When a couple of businessmen get together it's understood that unnecessary expenses have to be cut. It was stupid carrying a deadweight like Clip Haley.

Red McMann on the Spotter's orders had been clearing out the chiselers in the territory the Badgers had carved out for themselves (with brass knucks, fists, and the threat of guns) in Hell's Kitchen. That night, as he explained to Bughead Moore and Dutch Yaeger, they were paying a little visit on a couple of mutts. "This cheap mutt Donnelly thinks he can muscle in. Him we'll lump. An' there's this wop Rossetti peddling dago red which is okeh but the bastid won't pay protection. Him we'll give another chance."

An eye peered behind the door of the speakeasy run by Donnelly. It had a voice, small and snuffly as if it belonged to a guy with a cold: "What d'yuh want?"

"A drink," Red McMann said, gesturing at the two strongarms behind him, the Bughead and Dutch. "Just a li'l drink like we usta over at the Irish Harp."

The Irish Harp had been a corner saloon on Forty-fourth and Ninth with a stringless harp over the bar.

"Anybody from the Irish Harp," the snuffler said, unlocking the door.

The three Badgers pushed inside. The snuffler edged away. He was scared stiff, but his face revealed no emotion.

"Donnelly, yuh bastid!" the redhead grinned, grabbing the man's elbow and pulling him down the hallway into the front room. There, a half dozen customers sat with their drinks at a mixed lot of tables, none of them alike, as if purchased from a junk dealer.

A poor man's speak, Donnelly's. No big spenders came here. Neighborhood boys all of them.

They were scared, too, but Donnelly was doing the

sweating. Sweating blood, Dutch thought. He felt sorry for Donnelly. It was plain that the guy was just about scratching out a living.

"Hit the bricks!" the redhead ordered the customers with a friendly grin that proved he had no hard feelings.

When the last one had gone Donnelly wiped his sweaty face with the sleeve of his jacket. The Bughead laughed, reached into his pocket and flung a crumpled handkerchief into the man's face.

"Doncha say we don't give yuh nothin'!" the Bughead laughed.

Dutch winced to hear him. He stared down at the handkerchief. It wasn't clean. It was dirty. Snotty, he thought, feeling a little sick.

"Okeh," Donnelly muttered like a condemned man.

"Okeh," Red McMann mimicked. "Runs a speak in our territory an' its okeh."

"That isn't what I meant. I can't 'ford to buy your booze. This is a one-man proposition."

"A rathole," Red McMann agreed. "Sure yuh run a rathole but yuh pay the cops, right?"

"Who don't pay the cops?"

The redhead turned toward his silent strongarms as if to say: No argument on that, everybody pays the cops. The Bughead grunted. Dutch licked the insides of his dry mouth.

"You're through, Donnelly!" the redhead said. "We'll let yuh off easy this time. Nex' time it'll be the morgue!" He hadn't signaled his strongarms, but like himself, they were on the move.

149

"Have a heart," Donnelly pleaded when the wall stopped his backward retreat. "For Christ's sake—" he was saying when the redhead's fist caught him on the jaw.

Red McMann stepped back, examined his knuckles. The Bughead slugged the speakeasy owner. Dutch walloped one into the belly but he pulled his punch. As the redhead looked on like some referee, the two strongarms worked away like pick-and-shovel laborers, their fists their tools. Donnelly slumped, fell. Blood trickled from his mouth, curling like red worms on his chin.

The Bughead walked to one of the tables, picked up a bottle, sampled the whiskey, grunting as he spat it out. "Shit, it's half water."

The redhead led the way into the kitchen. The kitchens, as he knew, were the storerooms of two-bit speaks. He opened the doors of the closets. Light glinted on the round glass bellies of a dozen whiskey bottles. Seizing two in his freckled hands, he smashed them against the faucets in the sink.

The Bughead emptied the icebox. There were three gallon-jugs of home-brewed beer. He struck them with his blackjack. The nose-clinging smell of beer mingled with the sharper whiskey fumes.

The Bughead was returning to the front room when Red yelled to come back. The big blond head pivoted. For a second the Bughead's pale eyes, seemingly stuck to his face like two blue hunks of chewing gum, focused in a blind stare.

"Where the hell was yuh goin'?"

The Bughead jabbed a thumb at the front room.

"What for?"

"I was gonna boot him—"

"Boot him, yuh bastid?" the redhead cried. "The guy's been teached a lesson! Yuh don't beat a dead hoss!"

Dutch yawned awake in the furnished room he shared with Georgie. "Hey, Sleepyhead!" he called. "I'm hungry!"

Georgie kept on sleeping.

The guy was fooling around with some dame, as Dutch knew. But who she was and what her name was Georgie kept to himself. You'd be surprised, he'd teased Dutch. She's a raving beauty.

Dutch felt no envy. He had no complaints these days. True, some of the strongarm stuff gave him a queer feeling. Beating up speakeasy owners like Donnelly wasn't exactly fun, but every Friday, whether he worked or not, he got his fifty bucks in Cleary's back room.

The saloon up front, on Quinn's advice, was out of business; the Badger hangout had to look legit. The gilt letters on the plate glass—CLEARY'S SALOON—had been redone. CLEARY'S ASSOCIATION was what they said now. Above the window a brand-new sign had been hung, informing any passerby that this was also the YOUNG DEMOCRATS CLUB. If nothing else, Quinn believed in politics.

The thrill of being a Badger hadn't worn off for Dutch, swigging a beer in the back room with the gang, listening to the jokes. He belonged! A Badger was a Badger, even if he was a dutchman or a wop or a jewboy like Joey Kasow. And if he had bad dreams some nights, well, that's how it was. Awful dreams in which he was the guy being pounded into a pulp. . . .

Fifty bucks! Fifty iron men every Friday!

151

No more working for a dog's wages at Wortsman's stinking cheese store, no more getting up at seven in the morning. That was for suckers. But sometimes when he passed a bunch of kids playing Red Rover or Johnny Jump the Pony he would wonder how his brother and sister were doing. Easy for Georgie to cut himself loose from his family. An only child, Georgie. But Dutch had a kid brother and kid sister, and even if his old man was a creep, his old lady was okeh. Sometimes he'd ask Georgie— that Georgie knew everything!—about Paulie and Angie.

"Paulie," Georgie had replied, "will have to get a steady job unless he changes his mind about the charity ward for his mother. . . . Angie? He'll end up like his old man, fixing shoes all day, just a dumb wop. But Paulie—I hate to see Paulie chasing nickels. He's smart and you can trust him."

"Me, too," Dutch said, smiling as he thought of the back-yard shed and the pirate ship Paulie had carved with its flag lettered 1-4-All. . . .

EIGHTEEN

THE Spotter stood at the window of his room in the
Hotel Berkeley looking at the rain ricocheting from the
tops of the cars in the procession moving slowly toward
Sixth Avenue. The Spotter was not a rain-watcher. He
reflected that it must be his conscience bothering him.
Clip Haley, after all, had never done him any harm, and
here he was planning his funeral. He shuddered inside his
bathrobe whose rainbow colors matched the bright fronts
of the restaurants and chow mein parlors below, and
turned toward the warmth of his room as if a fire were
burning in the middle of the carpet.

Clip had to go, the Spotter thought, and Babyface
Georgie was just the lad to speed him on. He glanced at
his wristwatch. Georgie was due in ten minutes. The Spotter dressed, pulled on a pair of blue trousers with a narrow
white stripe, laced his black shoes, selected a white shirt
from the stack inside his top dresser drawer. Custom-made,
all his shirts, the monogram *B* stitched on the pocket.

There was a knock on the door. Georgie, his cap soaked,
his raincoat dripping rivulets on the carpet, stepped into
the room.

153

"You look like Noah's flood," the Spotter said. "Hang your stuff in the bathtub."

When Georgie walked out he wiped a stray raindrop from the tip of his nose, smiling as if the downpour in the street was another April shower. The Spotter waved a bony hand at a chair.

"Take a load off your feet," he said. "I'll get right to the point. Last week a guy by the name of Hatton came to see me. He sits down where you're sitting, two mugs with him to prove he means business. 'Spotter,' he says. 'I'm your new partner. It's going to be a fifty-fifty split from now on. Take it or leave it.' The two mugs they say nothing, but the next thing you know they pull a couple guns from their jackets. 'Think it over,' Hatton says. 'If it's war you want you'll get it.' I stalled around. He says, 'I'll give you a week.' 'Make it two,' I says. 'It's a deal,' the bastid says and walks out with his gunmen."

Georgie listened with the intensity of someone with faulty hearing.

He must be wondering, the Spotter thought, at all this inside stuff. "Why you, huh?" the Spotter smiled. "A new guy in the gang? I'll tell you why, Georgie. You happen to be smart, like Red McMann or Joey Kasow. Now to get back to Hatton. Hatton's a front for one of the biggest bootleggers in town. Ownie Madden. We found that out through Quinn's fat-ass Tammany pals. Quinn's for calling Hatton's bluff, if it is a bluff. Clip, I don't have to tell you how he thinks. Easy come, easy go. That's Clip. The hell with that! We got guns too!"

Georgie thought of the talk the Spotter had given him back in the winter. Speaks had to be protected, the Spotter said, and opening his address book he'd explained that he knew a fellow with a shooting range in his basement out in Brooklyn; a retired cop and part-time fence. The Badgers had done business with him before Prohibition. Twice a week Georgie had taken the subway to Brooklyn, the ex-cop instructing him how to handle a .38. In the beginning his bullets had missed the concentric numbered circles, but after a while he was scoring 6s and a few 7s. When he put his first bullet into the bull's-eye, the ex-cop had said: "You'll make a shot, not like some of those cockeyed Badgers. No goddam good unless you give 'em a sawed-off shotgun."

If Georgie was upset or worried by the Spotter's confidences, there was no guessing. His face was a closed mouth. The little bastard, the Spotter thought with grudging admiration. All set to knock off Hatton.

Rising from his chair, the Spotter walked to the dresser and opened a drawer, glancing down at the green paper filling it. Paper! With the easy money pouring in, that's all it was. He picked up a bundle of twenties, slipped off the rubber band. "I figure you could use a li'l extra, Georgie. How about a couple hundred?"

"Whatever you say, Spotter."

"That's a smart answer and it gets you an extra century."

He counted off fifteen twenties, which he put on an end table. "Don't forget to take 'em with you when you go," he grinned.

For some reason the Spotter's joke sent a shiver down Georgie's back. Something was fishy. Fishy from the start. Why pick on him to get Hatton when there were guys like Red and Joey? Why him, when all he'd ever shot at was a bull's-eye in a basement? He felt afraid and he hated himself for that. It was as if another Georgie had shown himself, a Georgie he didn't recognize. . . .

"I don't even know what Hatton looks like—" Georgie began.

"You know what Clip looks like!"

The Spotter might have been talking about the spring weather, but what he said ripped through Georgie like a bullet fired at short range.

The Spotter sensed it although there wasn't a dent in Georgie's poker face. "What's the matter kid?" he asked innocently.

"First it's Hatton—"

"It's both of 'em, Georgie. We got plenty guys to take care of Hatton. Clip, though, is made for you."

"Made for me?"

The Spotter smiled as he got ready to slap down his ace. "I got to hand it to you, Georgie. Who's been laying Clip's broad? Some other guy?"

"I don't know where you heard—"

"Heard it from Millie herself, so quit bullshitting, kid! Millie came to see me, crying her head off how you bamboozled her with that pocketbook you snatched. How if she didn't come across you'd run to Clip how she was holding out on him."

The Spotter's eyes, that ordinarily had as much expression in them as those in a stuffed fox, were shining now. "Clip's a woman chaser," he continued. "But Millie's still his girl. It's a good thing he doesn't know about you, Georgie. You still—"

"I haven't been near Millie in months," Georgie broke in before the Spotter could finish his sentence.

"To get back to Clip—"

Georgie flicked his thumb at the three hundred on the end table. "I don't want that kind of money."

"What's the big idea?"

"You're holding that broad over my head!"

"Wrong! It just happens I can do you a favor and you can do me a favor—"

"Some favor!" he burst out, unable to control that other Georgie who had slipped inside his skin.

"Wrong again, kid!" the Spotter said, as if he had been unjustly maligned. "Didn't I keep my mouth shut about you and Millie? Why? Because you're one guy with something more'n birdseed between your ears. I saw it when Red McMann brought you and that dutch sidekick of yours to Quinn in the old days. The Badgers need guys like you. It's a new time, and deadheads like Clip don't fit. You've got me all wrong, Georgie. I thought you was ready for anything."

"I am, but this—"

"This what? Here you were ready to go after Hatton, a guy with two mugs guarding him. Clip's a sitting duck. It's a favor to you and a favor to me."

It was also blackmail, but Georgie kept that thought to himself. He said: "I guess you're right, Spotter."

When he left the Hotel Berkeley, the three hundred in his wallet, he headed for the Automat on Broadway like a homing pigeon. He knew no one there, and no one knew him. The faces chewing sandwiches or sipping coffee could have been formed out of the same opaque material as the white-tiled tables.

He tossed his raincoat on an empty chair, stirred his black coffee. His cup might have been a crystal ball in which the future revealed itself, but unclearly, the Spotter's words ringing in his ears—*a favor to you and a favor to me....*

The tricky bastard, Georgie thought. Go believe him.

"Christ!" he muttered despondently. He dipped his spoon into his coffee. His hand trembled like an old man's and he stared at it as if it belonged to that other Georgie: the Georgie who wasn't sure of anything.

No matter what he did, the Spotter had him cornered. Clip had his friends in the gang, and all the Spotter had to do was spill the beans. *Yeh, that bastard Georgie killed Clip, and all for a cheap broad....*

What should he do? Believe the Spotter? Might as well believe in Santa Claus.

A sick grin touched Georgie's lips as he thought of the make-believe California where he was supposed to be. Maybe he ought to blow out with the three hundred bucks? Maybe take his chances? He couldn't decide, his head a racetrack without any sure winners.

Maybe he ought to talk it over with Dutch? No, he thought. He could trust Dutch all right, but in some ways Dutch could never see the difference between his ass and his elbow. And Dutch wasn't the only one. Here he was, the smart guy so-called, not so smart any more.

Noon found him waiting for Paulie at De Witt Clinton High School. The rain had stopped, the sidewalks sparkling in the spring sun. He looked at the crowds of students hurrying down the stone stairs and listened to the shouts of where-you-going-to-eat with a contemptuous smile. The same old jerks, he thought. Jerks, maybe, but at least they didn't have a knife at their throat.

"Hey, Paulie!" he called, and tried to smile.

"I'll be damned!"

"Didn't expect to see your Uncle Georgie? Throw those homemade sandwiches away! We'll have us a feed."

He suggested an Italian restaurant on Columbus Circle, but Paulie said the cafeteria was good enough. So once again, as if he'd never left school, Georgie ordered a plate of franks and beans. Had he seen the Spotter a few hours ago? In this eating joint the talk was about Clinton: the baseball team, the teachers. There was no Spotter talking out of two sides of his mouth. No Clip Haley, no Millie. Yet that wallet of his with three hundred bucks in it was proof enough that he didn't belong here.

Lowering his voice, he told Paulie about his talk with the Spotter. One, two, three! No beating around the bush! Paulie couldn't speak, staring at Georgie as if he'd never seen him before, an absolute stranger.

"It's me," Georgie said sarcastically. "No kidding, Paulie. It's me!"

He had already guessed what Paulie's advice would be, known it all along. Knowing, too, that he'd come here for the simplest of reasons. To hear himself talk to somebody he trusted.

"I had to get it out of my system," he said.

"Georgie, you've got to quit that mob—"

"Christ, if you don't sound like that priest of yours!"

159

Taking out his wallet, he opened the fold. "Betcha you never saw a C-note? There's three of 'em, back to back!"

"Georgie, listen to me!" Paulie pleaded. "You think you know everything, but you don't—"

"Don't give me that crap, Paulie. What's it got you? Dutch's old job at the cheese store? Hell, you'd be better off working for the Spotter. Pays fifty bucks a week."

"I don't want that kind of money!"

"*You* don't, but you ain't me. Talking to you cleared my head. That bastard had me going nuts for a while, but I'll show him a trick he never dreamed of! I'll quit but not before I pull some real dough out of the bastard. All the dough I can get!"

"You're crazy—"

"Not crazy, kid. Smart! As long as Clip lives, I'm safe. Don't you see it, Paulie? Clip's my insurance!" He burst out laughing, so loud and wild a laugh that heads turned at the nearby tables.

When Georgie became aware of them he quieted. "There's real dough up in the old Spotter's room at the Berkeley and I know where he keeps it. A whole ton of it. . . ."

NINETEEN

DUTCH opened his eyes in the furnished room he shared with Georgie. He glanced at his wristwatch on the table alongside his bed; it was almost one o'clock. "Damn!" he said, pulling on his pants. Bare-chested and in sock feet, not wanting to wake Georgie, he crossed to the sink. He washed and then he squeezed a three-inch worm of shaving cream out of its tube. He shaved carefully, yet he nicked his chin. "Ouch!" he cried, splashing cold water on the cut to stop the bleeding.

The sight of blood had never bothered him, but this morning he stared at the thin red sliver, thinking about the job that night. "Damn," he muttered.

When Red McMann had spelled it out—a raid on the clubroom of the Hudson Dusters—Dutch wasn't the only one who felt like jumping out of his skin. For two days running the Dusters, not satisfied with their own territory in Chelsea, had inched into the borderline streets above Thirty-fourth, into Badger territory. Salesmen with brass knucks, roughing up the owners of the independent speaks who were either protected or else bought their bootleg from the Badgers. The Dusters, as Red McMann explained, had to be cut down to size. Why had the Dusters decided to move north? That Red didn't explain.

"Keep it between us," the Spotter had instructed his lieutenant. "It's that goddam Hatton eggin' them on!" Relations between the two mobs had been peaceful; Duster leader Mike Cronin was no power bug. "It's Hatton putting ants in their pants. Maybe if we slap 'em back, Mike Cronin'll pull in his horns."

The bleeding had stopped. Dutch pushed the raid out of mind; he washed the lather from his chin and jaws, examining his face in the mirror. That nose of his'd always be a snout, those lips of his'd always be too thick. His cheeks though'd flattened out, no longer round and fat. Somebody was better-looking!

Few Badgers dared say otherwise. Dutch Yaeger was big and tough, even bigger with the pearl-handled .38 he now owned. He, like Georgie, had traveled to the basement shooting range in Brooklyn.

He brushed some talcum powder on the nick. For a second he thought of his father stomping home at night, his pig-sticker's uniform stained with blood. "Damn!" he said again.

He was knotting a gaudy necktie when Georgie called to him. "Hey, dude, you going to a wedding?"

"Wish I was. That raid tonight—"

"Cold feet, huh? You're not the only one, Dutch. The Spotter gives the orders and we hop like monkeys."

Georgie lit a cigarette. It tasted lousy, he thought. Everything was lousy. That little idea of his to grab the dough up in Spotter's hotel room wasn't worth a nickel.

The dresser drawer was as safe as the U.S. Mint. The Spotter was taking no chances of being knocked off by Hatton. He'd moved into a double room at the Berkeley with Sarge Killigan for a bodyguard, and downstairs in the lobby for good measure Bughead or some other strongarm hanging around. All of which, Georgie felt, put him behind the eight ball. Only one thing was sure. The Spotter was aching to plant a funeral wreath on Clip's coffin. And as long as Clip lived, the Spotter would keep his mouth shut how a certain party had been fooling around with Mille. There'd be no squealing to Clip. The squealing would come later: to Clip's pals. Unless the Spotter really meant that line of his about a favor for a favor. Georgie shook his head as if to dislodge the thoughts tormenting him.

"What's the matter, Georgie? Yuh gotta headache?"

"That guy's slippery as an eel."

"What guy?"

"Who do you think? That Spotter bastid." He listened to himself as if the words out of his mouth had issued from a ventriloquist's dummy. What would Dutch say, he wondered, if he told him about the Spotter's orders to knock off Clip? Nope, he thought. Dutch wasn't the guy. Too dumb. Georgie's eyes, brown and shining like polished glass, darkened with self-mockery. He had fancied himself as being smart. Yeh, smart as Dutch, smart as the Bughead —all of them putty in the Spotter's hands.

He watched Dutch wiggle his feet into a pair of shoes whose yellowish leather was almost as bright as the spring sunshine outside the windows. Dutch, a light tan Stetson on his head, crossed to the dresser. He lifted a couple of shirts in the bottom drawer, picked up his .38, and then carefully, as if handling an object put together with toothpicks, slipped it inside the holster strapped under his armpit.

"Wish me luck, Georgie." Dutch smiled. It was the nervous smile of a little boy turning the corner of a block where he didn't belong, full of kids ready—all too ready!—to lump a stranger.

"Wish us both luck," Georgie answered.

Georgie lit a second cigarette when the door closed. The room was quiet, but not so quiet that he didn't hear the Spotter's voice . . . *it's a favor to you and a favor to me.* . . . Georgie cursed, flipped his cigarette into the sink. He stretched out on his bed and stared at the faces spinning inside his mind—the Spotter, Clip, Millie, Dutch, Paulie. . . .

"Get lost," he groaned, but there was no stopping the merry-go-round.

Dutch always felt better out on the street, but today, as he walked by the brownstones to the corner—a brownstone neighborhood, Chelsea unlike red brick Hell's Kitchen—he thought that here he was plumb smack in the heart of Duster territory. Leave it to Georgie, he thought, to live where nobody knew them. But somehow it didn't seem like such a hot idea with the Dusters' raid coming off that night.

He breakfasted in a German bakery on Ninth. Ham and eggs and french fries, topped by coffee and a slab of cheese cake. He ate slowly to kill time, but after a second coffee he slipped the quarter tip of a big sport under his crumpled napkin. Chewing on a toothpick he walked north, glancing at his reflection in the store windows. Not at his face, the way he used to do a million years ago going to his job at the cheese store. What he inspected now was the fit of his suit, the tan Stetson on his head. He tugged at the brim. That's better, he thought, wondering why he was so fussy. As if he were going out on a date and not a little party with the Dusters. True, it was a warning raid, no guns, no shooting. There would be axes to smash up furniture, not heads.

Red had told them: "It's that mug Hatton makin' trouble. There's a chance the Dusters'll backwater providin' there's no blood. . . ."

No blood, Dutch brooded unhappily. Sure, no blood. But Red had told them to pack their guns just in case.

"There's never no guarantees," the Spotter's lieutenant had said.

Near the corner a group of little girls was playing on the sidewalk. Dutch watched as one pitched the patsy—a piece of tin—onto the square numbered *1*. He smiled, reminded of his kid sister. Maybe he ought to drop by one of these days to see Gertie and his mother? *Yeh, mom,* he would say, *I'm back from California, and if yuh need a li'l money for the house* . . . He could drop by when his old man was at work at the slaughterhouse. Who the hell wanted to see him? But his mother and Gertie'd be a sight for sore eyes. Even his kid brother, Emil, the rat.

He hastened his step as if he were going home: the prodigal son who had left to seek fame and fortune in a California around the corner.

Two hours later he emerged from a movie, blinking at the daylight that had been shuttered out in the movie dark. He glanced at his wristwatch. Not even five o'clock! More time to kill! He decided to drop in on the Badger hangout, play a little cards, chew the fat; and then almost instantly he changed his mind. He didn't want to see the guys who, like himself, were slated for the raid tonight: Ted Griffin, Cockeye Smith, Billy Lennon. Some of them would be there sure as fate. Maybe even Red McMann himself.

He shuddered as he thought of Red. There was a guy with nerves of steel.

Dutch wondered what was wrong with him. Was he getting cold feet, as Georgie'd said back in their room? All he knew was that he no longer felt safe.

Maybe it had been the sight of the little girls playing patsy and the emotions they had stirred in him. Almost he had forgotten where he was going, only to realize that he had walked a long time. For there he was on the old block, hurrying by the old shoe shop. Behind the plate-glass window Angie was working, head lowered. Dutch sighed, feeling like a ghost. He glanced about him in disbelief when he entered his own house, peering down the hallway toward the flat where Paulie's family lived.

"Mama! Mama!" Gertie cried when Dutch stepped into the kitchen of his own flat. "Mama, it's Henry!"

Henry—the name once his—like some suit of clothes he had once worn enveloped him from head to foot. Was he wearing a tan Stetson, light yellow shoes? Yes and no. His kid sister flung her arms around him, and Mrs. Yaeger, weeping with joy, embraced them both. "My little boy," she repeated over and over again, stroking his hair and cheeks.

"I'm not a little boy!" Dutch protested.

His mother let go of him, and hands on her hips, looked him over. "Not efen a letter," she said reproachfully.

And as Gertie asked about California he began to answer his mother's questions. He had meant to write, but he was too busy driving a truck—yes, a truck—and that was how he had come home. They listened spellbound as he told them about the big truck he'd driven to New York. He blinked as he looked at their soft blond faces, his mother's almost as innocent as his kid sister's. They believed him, he thought sighing. They believed him because they loved him.

The kitchen with its cast-iron stove and spotless white curtains was transformed in his eyes. He couldn't have expressed what he felt, but if some supernatural voice had whispered *this is a holy place*, he would've nodded his agreement.

"How is Emil, mama?" he asked.

"He iss growingk big, like you. All my boys iss big!" She said it proudly, and it was only after she had talked for several minutes that she exclaimed: "Papa! You don't ask about papa?"

"How is papa?"

"Like alvays. *Der Arbeit*. Work, work."

"Mama, I must go—"

"*Nein!* Mus' go! Supper you vill stay. I make all vot you like—"

"I can't, mama. I must get back to the truck." And reaching into his pocket for his wallet he took out a ten-dollar bill.

"*Nein!*" she said firmly.

167

"Buy a present for Gertie. For Emil."

He had to return the bill, and although Gertie pleaded with him, clutching his arm, he gently disengaged himself. He kissed Gertie and kissed his mother, who tearfully muttered that this was not a visit but a heartbreak. To come and go like the wind.

"I'll be back," he promised at the door. "Say hello to Emil. To papa," he added. And in the corridor he wiped the tears from his eyes.

"We're gettin' close," said Red McMann. "Remember what I told you guys!"

The stolen car rolled down Tenth Avenue. Dutch was driving, the Spotter's lieutenant next to him, and in the rear Ted Griffin, Cockeye Smith, and Bill Lennon sat elbow to elbow. Under their feet on the floorboard were two axes.

It was nearly midnight; the stores were dark squares, the tenement windows dark rectangles, a few yellow bright where people were still awake.

A warning raid, no guns, no shooting: the axes to smash up furniture. Those were the redhead's very own words, but now they repeated themselves ominously inside Dutch's head. He felt Red's hand on his shoulder. A friendly squeeze that spoke a language of its own: *You're okeh, Dutch, just take it easy.*

Dutch nodded. He liked Red, who'd shown him the ropes on his first job, but this job had aroused other emotions. Red's nerves were made of steel. Dutch envied him, wishing he could be as cool.

"Turn left," Red directed.

The long golden fingers of the headlights plunged down the sidestreet, another brownstone street in Chelsea, with little flights of stone stairs leading up to dimly lit vestibules. They were all the same, but with the raid only minutes away, everything had become strange to Dutch. The sidewalks leading nowhere, the walls of the houses seemingly made out of cardboard as if a strong wind could blow them all down. He could feel the iron lump of his .38 under his armpit, and for once he was glad to be the guy at the wheel. It was anybody's guess as to what would happen. One of the Dusters might draw his gun and start shooting. . . .

"Turn on Nint'," Red said.

He shifted into second gear, the El pillars parading before him like so many immovable gigantic figures. With the back of his hand he brushed the sweat that had collected like some night dew on the tip of his nose.

"We're almost there," Red said. "It's that pool parlor. Dutch, yuh keep the motor runnin'."

He braked to a stop. Suddenly he was alone in the stolen car, watching the Badgers legging it fast toward a cluster of stores. All of them dark except the pool parlor, the Dusters' clubroom and hangout. Through its curtained window, yellow light sprayed out on the sidewalk, on the axes in the hands of Ted Griffin and the Cockeye. He knew that they would be covered by Red McMann's and Billy Lennon's guns, and if all went well they'd be rushing out in a few minutes.

The yellow plate glass of the pool parlor seemed to throb with a life of its own, to pulse like the heart beating inside his own chest. Dutch wiped his sweaty hands on his trousers, the ignition panel wavering in his sight; and as the four entered the pool hall he felt a silence vast and immense, shattered almost instantly as the axes he couldn't see split chairs and tables.

He flinched at the first shot, shoved the gears into first, gasped at a second shot, a third! *No shooting, huh!* He was waiting, trembling. Then, as if swept out on the sound of gunfire, three shadows raced toward the car while a fourth stood guard at the poolroom door.

"Stay where yuh are!" Dutch heard the gunman—it was Red—as the three shadows turned into the recognizable shapes of Ted Griffin, Cockeye Smith, and Bill Lennon. They sprang into the rear of the car.

"C'mon, Red!" the Cockeye yelled.

Red McMann fired another shot, sprinted to the car, jumped in, slamming the door shut. Dutch stepped on the gas, shifted into second, into high.

"One of those bastids had to reach for his gun!" It was Red talking.

Had he killed the Duster? Whatever, it didn't matter, mattered even less when the piercing wail of a police car, like a sheet of metal ground into jagged shreds, ripped against their ears.

From the back seat Cockeye Smith shrilled a warning. Red cursed their tough luck. "A cruisin' cop! Speed it up, Dutch!"

"Faster, Dutch!" pleaded the Cockeye—or was it Ted Griffin or Bill Lennon? "Faster or we're done—"

His foot flattened the gas pedal, the El pillars now coming at him so thick and fast they seemed like a sliding wall.

"Get off the avenue, Dutch!" Red shouted.

The tires squealed as the car careened down a side street, the tenements on both sides no longer separate one from the other. Single-roofed, as if they had entered a street where two immense warehouses faced each other.

He must've hit a fallen box or a board in the gutter. Suddenly hands stronger than his own seized the wheel: hands without arms jerking out of the sleeves of uncontrollable speed. Sidewalks, tenements, the lights of the lampposts—a twisted and twisting ribbon whirled before him. The car slid across a gutter that seemed to be paved with ice, hitting a hydrant. Dutch's head snapped back like an apple tossed off a stick. Recovering from the shock, he spat blood from his mouth; his teeth had been knocked into his lips.

"Out! Out! Get out! You're on your own!" Red was · yelling, the police siren echoing his words, louder and louder, shrieking like a montrous beast mounted on wheels and closing in for the kill.

Dutch shook his head hard and stepped to the sidewalk, stumbling. He was unaware that Bill Lennon lay unconscious, sprawled on the rear seat, or that Red followed by the Cockeye, was sprinting toward the corner. Spitting blood, he darted into the hallway of a house, tugged at the vestibule door.

Locked!

That was all he knew.

He pulled out his gun, smashed the glass of the door, reached in through the splintered hole to turn the inside knob. As he rushed up the stairs he heard a voice shouting behind him, "Stop or I'll fire!"

He tried to shrink himself down in size. And although he wasn't as small or as quick as an alley cat, he made it to the landing of the first flight. The crack of the pistol he heard seemed louder than any El roaring down steel tracks. He ran to the second flight, deaf to the doors opening behind him, deaf to the voices of the excited tenants. All he saw were the endless stairs edged with brass. Without thinking, like a cornered animal showing its teeth, he glanced over his shoulder; only now was he conscious of the weapon in his fist. The smooth dead feel of the pearl-handled butt made him quiver as if a bucket of ice water had been flung into his face. He was fully conscious now that his life was on the line.

His life or the life of his pursuer.

He released the safety, the fear inside him screaming as if through a mouth of its own. He stopped his mad run, and when the dark blue shape of the cop appeared, he pulled the trigger. He knew that he'd missed when a bullet whistled over his head and buried itself in the wall.

His trembling body had reacted to the exchange of fire, his entrails opening up to discharge a load into his pants. He groaned as he realized what had happened.

He took the second flight, two stairs at a time. On the top floor he climbed a steep ladder, pushed the trapdoor open, the stars falling in a sudden white rain.

God, he wished, if I could only get away. Get away? Never!

It was as if even now Red McMann held him with arms

stronger than steel. Who but McMann had led Paulie and himself up to the roof of the Irish 1-4-Alls? Brought them to the Spotter? And now, when he most needed him, Red had run off like the rat he was, leaving him alone on still another roof. . . .

Jinxed, Dutch thought with superstitious anguish.

He rushed to one side of the trapdoor. Faraway he heard the sirens of the police cars summoned by the cruiser. He couldn't believe he was cornered, a gun in his fist, spitting blood out of his mouth.

"Jinxed," he muttered helplessly.

He might have tossed the gun aside if the cop's head and shoulders hadn't emerged through the trapdoor. Instead, he squeezed the trigger, or rather the fear inside him squeezed the trigger. The black shape spun around. It should have dropped from the ladder, but to Dutch's horror the cop clambered up on the roof, a black and frightening ghost, voiceless except for the pistol in its hand.

Two small slugs pierced Dutch. Small slugs, but they pounded away like hammers, sharp-edged, and more destructive than the axes that had wrecked the Dusters' hangout. They battered the insides of Dutch's stomach. Ceaseless blows drummed against his temples.

The wounded cop crawled across the roof, dragging his torn shoulder. Dutch saw no cop, no night, no stars. Blood trickled from his mouth on to the necktie he had so carefully knotted in his room before leaving. He was unaware of the blood, he didn't hear the voice—it was his own voice —the voice of a child moaning one word over and over again: *Mütter, mütter . . .*

173

The cop listened. He lay his pistol down on the roof, pulled out his flashlight, and stared at the dying boy's face. His nostrils dilated as he inhaled the stink of excrement. The bastard, he thought, could've killed me.

"*Mütter . . .*"

A kid, a baby in diapers, the cop thought with a grudging pity.

TWENTY

THE raid had cost the Badgers two good men. Billy Lennon, knocked unconscious when the stolen car crashed, had ended up in the hospital, facing a trial and a stretch in jail once he recovered. But Billy was lucky, as many a Badger remarked. No trials, no jails awaited Dutch Yaeger. "Pushin' up the daisies," they said of him.

The day after Dutch was killed, his mother found an envelope containing two one-hundred dollar bills and a penciled note in her letter box:

> *We join you in mourning your son.*
> *The enclosed is for funeral expenses.*

It was signed simply, *From some friends.* It proved, as the Badgers said, that the Spotter had a heart. Even in the middle of a gang war the Spotter, as Red McMann declared, had time to do the decent thing.

After the funeral everybody agreed that Mrs. Yaeger had been very brave, unlike Mr. Yaeger. "Look at him," the mourners whispered. "Carryin' on like a baby, that big strong man."

It was Mrs. Yaeger, a black shawl around her head, who had notified their relatives and some of the neighbors on the block. She wept only when she called on the parents of her dead son's closest friends.

"I know how you feel," Mrs. Alston had said tearfully. "Georgie— He might as well be dead for all we know."

Mrs. Alston had stayed away from the graduation party at the shoemaker's house, but she came to the funeral with her husband. Together with Mr. Cuomo and Mrs. Bolkonski they formed a self-protective cluster, bound together by memories of happier days when their sons had played together. Angie, side by side with Paulie, broke down when the dirt was shoveled into Dutch's grave.

For Paulie, that day had no beginning or end, like the day of his father's funeral. Dutch's death was terrible, but almost as bad was the burden Paulie carried. He alone knew what "friends" had sent the two hundred dollars for funeral expenses.

It wasn't only thoughts of Dutch that kept him from sleeping nights. Georgie, wherever he was, had reached out a long hand. "I ought to talk to the poor guy," Paulie said to himself. "I ought to . . ." He had no idea where Georgie lived, but he hadn't forgotten what Georgie'd said about the Badgers' hangout: *If I'm not at Cleary's they'll know where to find me.*

But what was the use, Paulie told himself in the morning with the fatalism, the street knowledge, of the poor. Georgie quit the Badgers? Never! A gangster was a gangster. Yet, as he walked to school these May mornings, the sunlit store windows, the flashing flags of spring itself, he wasn't so sure. Why not give it a try? Only to change his mind again when he hurried home. One day, as he approached the door he had painted yellow, he remembered how puzzled Dutch had been. *Why yellow?—It's the color of the flowers where my mother comes from, the color of the stuff they make bread out of.* . . . The old dialogue echoed in his head, voices out of a long-gone year when he and Dutch and Georgie and Angie had been kids playing in the backyard.

The retired nurse Dr. Reich had recommended smiled as Paulie entered the kitchen. "She is doing fine," the nurse said.

Paulie kissed his mother, and for a second that kiss dispelled all his doubts. What could he do? Go to the cops and holler: *The Spotter killed Dutch, the Spotter's after Georgie! Do something! Bust up the mob.* . . . Fat chance! They'd boot him out of the station house and serve him right for being a prize fool.

That night after supper he was unable to study, the print in his textbook a meaningless squiggle. It was almost like every other evening, the family gathered together in the kitchen, the supper dishes washed and dried by his sisters, the wall clock ticking away the minutes, Christ suspended on His cross in a timeless eternity.

Ava was writing in her notebook; Christina was reading, her pink lips shaping the words. He was overwhelmed by their innocence, crushed by his own helplessness. Maybe he ought to talk to Angie? For what? Because they'd once been 1-4-Alls? Angie would only parrot his old man. Talk to Mary! Mary loved him, and she was as smart as she was beautiful. Tomorrow, he thought with relief. Tomorrow he'd meet Mary after school.

Girls by the hundred, giggling, chattering, walked through the wide open doors of Washington Irving High into the golden light of a spring afternoon.

"Mary!" he called. "Mary!"

"Paulie!"

She was surprised to see him. They never met on Tuesdays.

"There's a reason, Mary," he explained. "It's about Georgie. 'Bout Dutch, too. I mean, I can't get them out of my mind—"

Incoherent at first, he forced himself to slow up. "Lissen," he began again. And as he spoke he felt as if the burnished avenues they were crossing had widened into an incalculable distance and that she was on one side with her father and brother, and with his own mother and sisters, while Georgie and Dutch were on the other. Even before he finished he knew what she would say.

No mistaking the fear and alarm in her eyes.

They had cut through the park at Union Square with its statue of George Washington mounted on his horse, Fourteenth Street with its big stores before them.

"Well?" Paulie asked.

"Well what?" she said sharply. "You mustn't!"

"Mustn't, huh? I tell you I can't get 'em out of my mind!" His heart ached, and on a tide of memory he was swept back into a candlelit shed, Georgie and Angie and Dutch and himself sitting together as 1-4-Alls, sworn to stick up for one another. . . .

She seized his hand. "Paulie," she pleaded. "You'll only get yourself into trouble—"

"Georgie came to me an' you want me to let him down!"

"He did the letting down, Paulie! He joined the gang, not you!"

"An' what about poor Dutch? I'm not goin' to let 'em get away with murder!"

"Sh! Sh, Paulie! Do you want the whole street to hear you?"

"I tell you—"

"Paulie," she whispered. "Dutch was killed by a cop, not by one of those gangsters—"

"The same thing!"

"It's not the same, Paulie. They joined the Badgers, they wanted to join, didn't they?" She stared at his clenched lips. "Paulie, you can't, you mustn't get mixed up! Paulie, promise!"

"I'm promisin' nothing!"

After supper he again was unable to concentrate on his homework. Mary was right, why look for trouble? If he stuck his nose in, what would happen to his mother, his sisters? Who'd take care of them?

It took him a long time to fall asleep that night. He buried his face in the pillow, but Georgie followed him there. And once again he was rushing up the stairs—the last flight Dutch would ever climb—side by side with Dutch and on the roof waiting for them with drawn guns—not the cops, but the Badgers.

"I'm glad you decided to talk to me," Father McGinley said when Paulie finished. The sun poured through the windows of his office at Holy Cross, but bright as it was, the priest felt as if the blond boy had brought with him the darkness of the gang-infested streets of Hell's Kitchen.

"We got to do something!" Paulie said.

"I know how you feel about your friends, Paul. When I think of the kids recruited into the Badgers by the likes of Red McMann and Spotter Boyle my heart breaks. Enough of that! We've got to do something! Let me think, Paul. We could talk to Hearn. If there's one honest Tammany alderman, it's Hearn the undertaker."

Late that afternoon they stepped into the undertaker's street-front establishment. The partitioning wall had been removed between two stores; a handsome oak door opened on the rear where the dead were prepared for burial. The door was closed. Just the same, Paulie averted his eyes from the casket on display. It was empty, but he couldn't help thinking of Dutch in his coffin. Quiet and unnatural, like a man-sized doll.

"Mr. Hearn, this is Paul Bolkonski, and as I said when we spoke on the telephone, he has something important to say."

The undertaker smiled. Big and red-faced, he didn't look like an undertaker. But Paulie, glancing at his square, short-fingered hands, wondered how many corpses had passed through them. He turned his head and peered at the potted rubber plants.

"I'm listenin', Paul," Hearn said.

When Paul finished Hearn shook his head. "That's how it is in Hell's Kitchen. Some go straight like you and others end up in the gangs. This Georgie Alston, if I get you right, is gunning for Clip Haley? That doesn't surprise me. Spotter's a mean one. I shouldn't say it, a God-fearin' man like m'self, but I hope Spotter gets what's comin' to him before this bootlegger's war's over! Paul, let me say this. This German boy Yaeger—too bad about him, but he could've killed that cop. Too bad he had to die so young, but bullets have no age. He could've killed that cop who was only doin' his duty."

"Mr. Hearn," Father McGinley pleaded with him. "That's all true, but the point is, what can be done now?"

"Son," the undertaker addressed Paulie. "You said you're willing to talk to the police about what this Georgie Alston told you?"

Paulie nodded.

"Ah, you're a brave lad but I'm afraid we'd get nowhere. The Spotter has his connections, good connections. He'd deny the whole thing, and remember, it's no secret that the cops like nothing better than to see the gangs shooting at each other. Take my advice, son, and keep your skirts clean."

"That's all you hear!" Father McGinley exclaimed. "And it's not good enough!"

Hearn sighed. "It's not all that simple, Father. Now if you could get the goods on the Badgers—"

"Goods?" the priest asked.

"Evidence that'd hold up in a court. Criminal acts. Proof they're breakin' the law. Proof they're sellin' bootleg. Better yet, proof that in this bootleg war some Badger put a bullet in one of the mobsters they're fighting. Homicide! If there's proof of homicide the police'll act."

"Georgie!" Paulie cried.

The two men stared at him, and then the undertaker shook his head. "Son, from what you've said about this Georgie, I have my doubts that he'd be any help—"

"Suppose he told the cops all he knows about the Spotter? Suppose he told 'em how the Spotter wants him to kill Clip Haley?"

"It'd be his word against the Spotter's—"

Father McGinley pounded his fist against the palm of his hand. "At least that would be a start—"

"Excuse me, Father," Hearn said quietly. "But you're dreaming. Georgie'd be taking his life in his hands if he went to the cops."

"He could be protected," the priest said. "The church was a sanctuary in bygone centuries for the persecuted, for all seeking safety from the lawless—"

"Excuse me, Father," Hearn said as quietly as before but with an ironical smile on his lips. "You have a nice sermon there to preach of a Sunday, but from what I've heard about this Georgie he's not the type to take his life in his hands—"

"I could talk to him!" Paulie interrupted.

"Sure, son, if it'll make you feel better." And, still smiling, Hearn shook his head as if he had been listening to two children.

CLEARY'S ASSOCIATION
YOUNG DEMOCRATS CLUB

Paulie peered at the gilt lettering on the plate-glass window, duplicated in a red, white, and blue sign mounted

above the curtain. He blinked. He clenched and un-
clenched his fists before opening the door. Inside, in the
space once a saloon and now an oversized vestibule leading
into the back room, there were still other changes. An
American flag draped one wall. The governor of New York
and the mayor of New York City smiled out of large
photograhps.

("If we're a-goin' to call ourself an Associayshun an' a
Young Democratic Club," Tom Quinn had counseled the
Spotter, "then by George we owe it to ourself to look
Democratic." "Camouflage?" said the Spotter. "Politics,"
said Quinn.)

The door to the backroom was ajar. Paulie couldn't see
the poker players or the drinkers having themselves a snort.
Now and then a single voice lifted in a curse or a shout.
Paulie flushed as if they were all howling at him. He ad-
vanced slowly, cautiously, like a boxer appraising a heavier
and stronger opponent in a ring.

A dozen faces confronted him.

"I'm a friend of Georgie Alston—"

"Yeh?" someone jeered. "What the hell d'yuh want?"

"Georgie said you could tell me where he lives. I've got to
see him."

"Sez yuh!"

One of the poker players laughed. "Yuh think this punk's
wunna the Hatton mob? Beat it, punk!"

"It's important—"

"No tickets, no addresses," a joker hollered.

"It's important—"

"Okeh. Tell yuh what, punk. We'll gi' him the word."

"Thanks. Tell him Paulie wants to talk to him."

"Jus' that?"

"Yes. Paulie from the old block wants to talk to him."

"Okeh, Paulie," the joker said. "We'll tell'm Paulie Blockhead wants-a talk to him."

TWENTY-ONE

NOBODY gave Georgie *the word* about Paulie. Even if there hadn't been a war with the Hattons, no Badger would've gone against Red McMann's orders: "Keep your traps shut about the guys in this bunch!" They were the Spotter's orders, too, and his lieutenant echoed them, almost unable to conceal the pleasure he took in his new authority.

Georgie was the only Badger, outside of a couple of fighting fools like the Bughead, who wished that the gang war started by Hatton would go on forever. As long as it lasted, Georgie was off the hook. He could almost forget the three century notes the Spotter had handed him with Clip Haley's name printed on each as if in invisible letters. There was no more talk of getting rid of Clip. All the talk was of Hatton, that mad dog, who'd encouraged the Dusters to move north. The Dusters had called off the war after Quinn's Tammany connections had met with the politicians who represented the citizens of Chelsea: good citizens and citizens not so good. Hatton, though, was something else. He had phoned the Spotter, cursed the peacemakers, and promised the Spotter a piece of lead in the back if he wasn't cut in on a fifty-fifty split.

"What the hell are you, a mad dog?" the Spotter had answered.

To which Hatton had agreed with a laugh: "Sure, you no-good bastid."

Not a word of this conversation leaked down to the gang. The Spotter had only passed it on to Red McMann. The gang was told to get ready for anything. The bouncers in the sixteen Badger speaks, who had trusted their muscle, now all packed guns under their armpits.

"The bastids've got to come to us," Red McMann said, repeating the Spotter's words. "An' when they do we'll blow hell outta them!"

A sound strategy, but the Hattons had the advantage of mobility. There wasn't a day (or night) when some Badger speak wasn't wrecked, the customers driven into the street. One armed bouncer was no match for four or five Hattons spraying gunfire. True, quite a few Hattons had been wounded or killed, but the Badger death toll was larger— Billy Muhlen, Ted Griffin, and three others.

Georgie had been assigned to back up Limpy Malone, the bouncer of one of the biggest Badger speaks that so far hadn't been hit. Like some soldier in combat, Georgie could think only of his own skin. But there was no forgetting Dutch. Georgie had tried to bury his old pal a second time, to push him into the darkest and most secret corner of his mind—deeper than any grave where a hundred unwanted memories were piled up in a dusty heap.

The day after Dutch's funeral Georgie had moved out of the furnished room they'd shared. Dutch's clothes he sold to a secondhand dealer. He felt cheap, but there was no sense leaving them for the landlady. He had rented a single room, and as he hung up his suits in the closet—he was a quiet dresser—he couldn't help thinking of Dutch's glad rags. Luck, he brooded, and his was all bad. Even if he pulled through, the Spotter still had him by the throat.

"The saints're watchin' over us, Georgie," was Limpy's devout comment. "It's like the Hattons don' know we exist. Clip's for throwin' in the sponge. Even Quinn's talkin' of dealin' in Hatton, but not the Spotter. That bastid'll hold out 'til we're all corpse meat."

"But suppose the Spotter gets knocked off?"

"Nah, Georgie! You're new inna gang. There's been a lot o' leaders an' where're they? Pushin' up the daisies or up in Sing Sing. Clip's holed up, but mark my woids, Clip'll get it before the Spotter."

He would remember that conversation when Hatton got himself shot dead, not by the bouncer guarding the speak where Hatton and three of his mugs put in a midnight appearance, but by Cockeye Smith of all guys. Cockeye, as he said himself, was just visiting. Georgie didn't know whether to be glad or sorry. He had a hunch that soon he'd be hearing from the Spotter.

Two days passed peacefully. Hatton's mob, their leader knocked off by a lucky bullet, had gone, leaving no trace, down the black rathole of the city's vast underground.

"Cockeye desoives a medal!" the Bughead shouted at the celebration party at Cleary's Association.

Sarge Killigan seconded the motion: "A bokay an' a medal."

The Spotter had already given the lucky marksman a hundred-dollar bonus, but as they tilted their glasses with real, genuine, unwatered, undosed, undoctored whiskey, he plucked a second century note out of his wallet: "This'll keep the other company, Cockeye."

Georgie bit on his lower lip as he remembered the extra hundred he himself had received one rainy day. And when the Spotter beckoned to him, he felt as if he'd never left the Spotter's room at the Hotel Berkeley.

"We still got some unfinished business, Georgie," the Spotter said with a little grin on his bony face. "Come see me at my hotel tomorrow, Georgie. At eleven."

When he'd gone, his bodyguard Sarge Killigan at his heels, Georgie heard him as if the Spotter's disembodied voice was afloat in the clouds of tobacco smoke . . . *a favor for a favor.* He refilled his glass at the improvised bar, listened with half an ear to the Bughead bragging how he'd kicked in the ribs of one of the Hattons: "Broke 'em into toot'picks!"

"Yeh, but we paid plenty," another Badger reminded the Bughead. "Don't forget Billy Muhlen, Ted Griffin, an' Dutch Yaeger."

Georgie's lips tightened to hold back the tears. Tears for Dutch or for himself? For both of them maybe.

It was past midnight when he left the celebration party, legging it down the long blocks to the single room where he'd moved after Dutch's death. Now and then he glanced up at the rooftops, as if Dutch's body were sprawled on each and every one. God, what am I going to do, he wondered. I've got to think of something or I'm done.

But that mind of his usually so quick and sure, seemed paralyzed. At eleven the next day he stood in front of the Spotter's door at the Hotel Berkeley. He glanced down the empty corridor and felt like running. But where? Trembling, he knocked and was admitted by Sarge Killigan.

The Spotter smiled, raised a limp hand. On one of the fingers a big diamond (the Spotter's gift to the Spotter now that Hatton was dead) caught the light. "Sarge," he ordered. "Leave us alone a minute."

Like a trained dog, the bodyguard stepped out into the corridor.

"This'll be short and sweet," the Spotter said. "Today's Thursday. I'm giving you 'til Tuesday of next week to do us both that li'l favor we spoke about."

"Tuesday?"

"That's when Clip sees Millie. See, we've been making it easy for you, Georgie. We've kept an eye on that yellow bastid. Where was he when the Hattons were knocking us off? Holed up in the Hotel Astor with his fancy broad. But now that things're quiet he's back to normal."

Georgie was silent.

The Spotter sized him up: "You can renege if you want, but if you do, you won't go far. And you got the brains to go far. Like Red McMann, for instance."

It was only yesterday when the Spotter had had a little confidential talk with Red McMann. He'd begun by pointing out that Clip had gone soft, predicting that Clip would fold if another mad dog like Hatton showed up. So why give Clip the chance? Why couldn't a guy like Red move up once Clip was out of the way? Not that he was asking

Red to take care of Clip. No, sir! And lighting a cigarette he'd spelled out the details of the *unfinished business*. Soft as Clip was, a mush pot, he'd put a bullet into the limey bastid if he ever found out how Georgie had wormed his way in with Millie. Georgie was the guy to take care of Clip, and once he did. . . .

The Spotter had paused, tapping Red McMann's knee: "We don't want him around neither, if you follow me. Between you and me, Red, the limey bastid's been conniving with the Dusters. That's why he lives down in their territory. So far I haven't got the goods on him, but who's to deny that there're guys who'd turn stool pigeon in a minute while other guys you could depend on like your own right arm. Like you, Red."

"I'm your man all the way, Spotter," Red said.

The Spotter smiled. "I've always known that, Red. We'll give Babyface 'til Tuesday. If he stalls, there's no guessing what he'll do. Join up with the Dusters maybe? Anyway, Clip we can take care of later. Babyface we can take care of on Tuesday if he stalls. . . ."

That little confidential talk was like the memory of a good dinner. The Spotter felt good. Hatton, Clip, Georgie. Yes, sir, he'd wipe the slate clean.

Now he smiled at Georgie. "Kid, if you've lost your nerve, say so and no hard feelings. Of course you'll have to return the three hundred bucks you got from me. But once a Badger always a Badger," he added as if swearing on a stack of Bibles.

"I haven't lost my nerve."

"You bet you haven't!" the Spotter declared. "If there

ever was a comer it's you, Georgie. I knew it from the minute I saw you."

On leaving the Spotter's room Georgie had himself a long think in a coffeepot. The only sure fact was Tuesday, and what about Thursday, Georgie asked himself. Thursday, Friday, Saturday, Sunday, Monday, Tuesday. He murmured the names of the days and was about to begin again when he stopped himself. Christ, people'd think he was one of those lame brains who went around the city talking to themselves.

What was the smart thing to do? Quit the gang? Or take his chances the Spotter was on the level?

Georgie stirred his black coffee, tasted it. It was cold, bitter. He pushed the cup away, and as the cup slid across the table, it turned into a snow-white train with himself on board, bound for California. Yeh, I can quit the gang, and Paulie'll give me a medal. Quit and go straight. Get two medals for that. And if I don't quit? If I knock off Clip—

He felt nauseous at the thought, as if he'd swallowed the bitter cold coffee in one quick gulp. Round and round his thoughts spun. And Georgie, biting on his lips, thought: I'm like a dog chasing its tail.

Trust the Spotter? Might as well trust a snake. Let's say I knock off Clip, then what? The Spotter would have me by the throat. Kill me another guy, and if I didn't, if I said I don't want to be a rubout man, all he'd have to do is pressure me with Millie. Have the bitch point a finger at me. Georgie killed Clip! I'd have to shut her up, kill her, kill the Spotter. Kill! kill! kill!

He groaned so loudly that people at nearby tables glanced at him. Georgie got up and walked out to the street.

Still Thursday, he thought. I'll think of something, he assured himself. And he knew he was deluding himself, like a kid whistling in the dark.

The next two days seemed as long as years to Georgie. Hat brim pulled low to hide his face, he tailed Clip Haley. Clip was living high, right smack on Broadway in the Hotel Astor, pushing through the revolving doors, a lightweight gray hat on his head, coming down with his fancy broad of an evening. Why Clip hung on to Millie was one of the seven mysteries, Georgie thought. The Astor broad was pretty enough to be in the movies, and Millie'd never been a prize-winner.

By the end of the second day Clip Haley had changed into a moving target, like the flat metal torsos in a shooting gallery. Shapes stamped out in a mill, painted white and topped by featureless faces. But this one didn't clank by on a metal track. This one knocked on the doors of the Badger speaks, this one stepped inside the door of the Badger hangout. This one—come Tuesday night—would climb the stairs of Millie's roominghouse. And if he knew that, why had he tailed him? Crazy, he thought. I'm going crazy.

Day and night Georgie was haunted by the Spotter, a bastard shelling out C-notes like so many cigar coupons, promising the big blue sky. And yet how could he believe him? As he tagged after Clip he left a trail of half-smoked cigarette butts, coughing as he killed a pack and with shaking fingers ripped open the silvery foil of a second, staring as the wind picked up the torn pieces and flung them down the sidewalk. There I go, he thought, as if he already felt the blast of the wind that had taken Dutch.

When he returned to his room it was like stepping into a Coney Island maze of mirrors where there were no exits. Knock off Clip? That could be his own death ticket. All the Spotter had to do was slip the word to one of Clip's pals, and if not the Spotter, Millie might tip them off. Millie hated him, and to be fair, Georgie thought, you couldn't blame her. But maybe the Spotter was on the level; maybe it was a favor for a favor? And wasn't that just what the Spotter wanted him to believe? Bait! Poison bait! And like some poor fish he was ready to swallow it.

He tossed himself down on the bed in his new room. Footsteps on the stairs outside brought him up into a sitting position. He listened to them ascending the next flight. No, it wasn't Dutch. It'd never be Dutch anymore. "Christ, Dutch," he muttered, "why'd you have to get yourself killed?"

And for a few seconds he mourned his old sidekick.

He had questioned all the others in on the Dusters raid: Red McMann, Ted Griffin, and Cockeye Smith. Billy Lennon, on ice in a prison hospital, there was no talking to. And now their replies burst inside his head like the voices of so many spooks: *Hell, when the car went outa control we knew we was in for it* (Ted Griffin talking before he was gunned down in the war with the Hattons) ... *It was each man for himself* (Red McMann talking) ... *I shoulda been at the wheel an' Dutch he'd be here today* (Cockeye the blowhard talking).

Georgie rubbed at his forehead. It felt hot, but he knew

he wasn't getting a cold. This was a different kind of fever.

Down in the street a truck rolled by, and there was Dutch, alive and well, at the wheel of the stolen car, Red McMann next to him and in the rear Ted Griffin, Cockeye Smith, and Billy Lennon. Driving to his death Dutch was, even if he didn't know it. Maybe that was what he was doing, Georgie thought, sitting at the wheel of a death wagon. The stolen car whirled across his mind, and in his fear it changed into a hearse, and he was inside it with Dutch and Ted Griffin. . . . With Billy Lennon in the hospital there was only Red McMann and the Cockeye still alive and kicking. And Red? He didn't count, Georgie thought superstitiously, as if the Spotter's lieutenant was actually a part of the Spotter, like a third arm. Leave Red out. There were just four in that car. One, two, three, four, like the 1-4-All Club.

Dutch was dead, he thought, and I'll be next, like Ted Griffin. Only Angie and Paulie are safe. . . .

TWENTY-TWO

Tuesday night Georgie sat waiting for Clip in a cafeteria on the corner of Millie's block.

Waiting, too, in a furnished room directly across the street from Millie's house, was Red McMann. He'd been there since late afternoon, like a hunter hidden behind a blind. A restless type, Red McMann, and although he had fortified himself with nips out of a bottle of rye, he was sick and tired of being cooped up. Every once in a while he cursed Georgie as a rat, Clip as a yellow-bellied bastard, Millie as a two-timing tramp. Cursed the Spotter, too, although he had no real complaints against him. Once Clip and Georgie were taken care of, he was all set, the Spotter's right arm!

Murder?

To Red McMann it was just another job. He had a gun under his armpit, a mask in his pocket purchased in a five-and-dime store and used on other jobs.

Georgie sat at a table near the window, his coffee and doughnut untouched; the *Daily News* was spread before him, the columns of print, the photos empty spaces, unread and unseen.

I could forget the whole damn thing, he thought miserably. Blow out. Blow out where? To the Dusters? Spill the beans about the Spotter's operations? They'd listen, but how far would I get? Nobody trusted a stool pigeon. Blow out to a job that paid peanuts? At least I'd be able to sleep nights. . . .

He had gone over the possibilities again and again, turned them all down. He could no longer think straight, and he knew it.

He walked to the counter for another coffee. "Black," he muttered, his eyes lowered, not wanting the counterman to remember his face, haunted by an image of Clip on a slab in the morgue, the cops buzzing the neighborhood for tips.

"Cream?" the counterman asked.

"No. Just black," he said and wondered why he was here in this cafeteria.

You're here, he answered himself, because you've got no other place to go. The thought struck him like a revelation, as if some fortune-teller reading his palm had deciphered the future out of a maze of meaningless lines. This cafeteria, for all its shining glass and white enamel, was a blind alley: the alley that had been his life.

Back at his table, he glanced through the window. A drunk staggered toward Eighth Avenue, passing the General Post Office, its vast white bulk looming like an iceberg, the stairs misty white. On those stairs, in a long-gone winter, he remembered racing down on his sled, steel runners sliding swift as light over the icy surface. Dutch shouting he could beat anybody . . . Paulie scuttling after them,

his sled a garbage-pail cover, the handle hammered flat. . . .
Poor Dutch was dead. A true friend, Dutch. A little dumb,
but a friend.

I was the smart one, Georgie thought bitterly. The trouble was that guys like the Spotter were smarter. . . .

An old man carrying a bowl of green pea soup sat down
at Georgie's table. Georgie lifted the *News* like a paper
screen between them, glanced at the wall clock. Almost
ten! And where was Clip? Maybe he wouldn't show? His
heart raced at the thought.

He flipped the *News* to the centerfold with its montage
of faces. Ugly some of them, powerful some of them, and
featured in the middle a beauty, her perfect face holding his
attention for a second when his eyes shifted to the street
outside the cafeteria window.

Clip!

It was as if one of the faces in the newspaper had slipped
through the glass. Georgie got up and walked out on the
dark sidewalk. Ahead of him were two men. The wind
blowing from the river carried their voices.

"Arnie recommended this speak . . . the real McCoy . . .
maybe but you know Arnie. . . ."

Georgie muttered a curse, but whether he was cursing
the pair blocking his view of Clip's broad-shouldered figure
or cursing himself he would never know. He restrained an
impulse to quicken his step. Nice and steady, he cautioned
himself.

Nice and steady. That had been his motto ever since
Millie had taught him the tricks of the shoplifter's trade.

At the end of the block an El streaked by in a yellow

blaze of light, vanishing in a second, leaving the street behind it dark and night-stilled for all its many noises. Heels tap-tapping, automobile horns honking.

The two men who knew Arnie entered a brownstone. With the abruptness of a vision the faceless body of Clip Haley, topped by a felt hat, appeared as if lifting out of a crack in the sidewalk. Georgie slowed his pace. The Badger leader mounted a flight of five brownstone steps— Millie's house! In the vestibule, the faceless head showed a profile.

Give him a minute to ring her bell, Georgie rehearsed what by now was a familiar role. A minute to unlock the door.

That minute turned into an hour, a year, eternity itself where nothing existed but a man fumbling with his keys. And in that eternity Georgie pitied Clip Haley, pitied himself. It was the realization that neither of them were free of the Spotter; robots for all their human hearts.

The vestibule door was opening—Clip was still a target! Georgie reached for the .38 in his pocket. His hand dropped. He was trembling, no longer knowing why he had spared Clip's life, or if he had known, he'd forgotten. That scheming head of his had emptied. All that remained was fear.

Fear had a face, and the face was the Spotter's.

As Georgie rushed down the block he was followed by Red McMann. A little wobbly in the legs, the redhead regretted the pint of rye he'd killed. Reneged! he thought. The limey bastard had reneged! Now where was he bound for? The Dusters?

He was tempted to pull out his gun and finish the job but there were too many people on that block with almost every second house a speakeasy.

Later, Red McMann told himself, I'll get him later. . . .

Georgie hadn't drunk anything but coffee. Just the same, he was as mindless as a slobbering drunk, his head clearing only when he reached Ninth Avenue where he turned north. Paulie! He whispered his friend's name, almost sobbing with relief.

The hour was late, the stores closed for the night; but as Georgie passed Thirty-fourth Street, he felt eased. Familiar stores: Rothenberg's Drugs, Voelker's Bakery, Fullan's pawn shop. He hurried past Thirty-sixth Street, where he'd gone to P.S. 32; legged past Thirty-seventh, the peppermint block where Paulie and Dutch had sneaked into the backyard of the Irish 1-4-Alls; and like a homing pigeon he rushed around the corner of Thirty-eighth, his old home block. It seemed like years since he'd set foot here.

"God," he muttered.

Following him, Red McMann was puzzled. Duster territory was down in Chelsea, not north in Hell's Kitchen. Who was the limey rat seeing on the q.t.? the redhead asked himself as he shadowed Georgie. A good thing he'd held fire, the redhead congratulated himself. A good thing. . . .

When Red McMann saw Georgie step into the vestibule of a tenement below the shoe repair shop a flash of memory bright as a searchlight shot across his whiskey-fogged mind. Wasn't this Dutch's house? And the house of that polack kid what's-his-name? The flash became intense, and in its light Red stood once again on a rooftop flying pigeons while down below in the backyard two boys ran around picking up peppermints tossed from the peppermint building.

He sprinted across the gutter, cursing himself as the inside door opened and closed. He was absolutely sure now what Georgie was up to. Bound for the Dusters he wasn't! Bound for the cops to spill the beans! Why else would the limey rat come to the house of that mama's boy, that lousy polack what's-his-name.

He squinted at the names on the letter boxes:

McAuliffe
Gruenzer, V.
Yaeger

His eyes focused on *S. Bolkonski;* that must be the polack. He wished that he'd gotten the limey while he'd had the chance. Should he ring the polack's bell or wait outside on the sidewalk? Nix on the bell, he decided. If he knocked Georgie off inside the house, even if he wore his mask, the polack might guess who he was from his build, his red hair. Sure, he was wearing a hat, but the mask didn't cover his sideburns or the back of his head.

He walked out to the sidewalk, thinking he'd get Georgie when he came out. But suppose he didn't come out, suppose he holed up for the night? Cripes! he cursed. Why hadn't he put a bullet into the rat while he'd had the chance. Chance, hell! With the booze in him he couldn't have hit a brick wall.

There was nothing to do but wait. He sat down to one side of the door, yanked the brim of his hat lower on his face. People going by—there were few at that hour—would think he was a drunk unable to keep his feet.

Red McMann grinned at his cunning, and like a hunter who had missed his first shot, he waited to get in a second. . . .

Georgie hurried down the hallway after ringing Paulie's bell, the vestibule door clicking open. He knocked on the painted yellow door of the behind-the-stairs flat, quivering when he heard Paulie's voice: "Who's there?"

"Me, Georgie."

The door creaked, and Paulie stared at his friend with unbelieving eyes.

"Paulie—Paulie, you got to help me! I don't know if I'm coming or going—"

Another voice, Paulie's mother. Georgie flinched as Paulie turned: "It's Angie, mama. I'll be right back."

"At this hour? So late?"

"I'll be right back, mama."

He stepped out, whispered: "Come, Georgie."

"I didn't do it, Paulie."

"You mean—"

"Clip."

Paulie flung his arm around Georgie's shoulders and without a word led the way to the cellar. They slipped in behind the door, side by side on the top stair. Faceless, both of them, in a darkness blacker than the coal in the bins below.

"Now we can talk," Paulie said. His breath quickened

and he exclaimed, "Gee, Georgie, I could kiss you!"

"I had 'til today but I couldn't do it."

"Thank God!" In his joy the cellar no longer stirred up memories of the raw grave in the cemetery where his father was buried.

"Paulie, I don't know where I'm at. 'You can renege,' he said, 'and you'll still be in the gang.' Go believe that snake! I'm scared sick, Paulie. I wish I'd never seen that snake!"

"Georgie, you mean it?"

"Mean what?"

"Quitting the Badgers?"

Paulie couldn't see him in the dark, but he felt Georgie trembling; they stood so close to one another. Again, he circled Georgie's shoulders.

"I got to quit or I'll be dead," Georgie mumbled. "Christ, I don't know what to do, Paulie."

"I know!" Paulie said. "We'll go to the station house—"

"The station house! The cops—"

"Yeh, the cops—"

"You crazy?" Georgie whimpered. "A stool pigeon! They'd kill me, Paulie! The Spotter—"

"He'd be in jail, Georgie—"

"You must be crazy—"

"I'm not crazy, Georgie. He'd be in jail because you've got the goods on him—how he wanted you to kill Clip. Georgie, you've got the goods on that bastid!"

Georgie was silent, breathing so hard it seemed as if he were talking in some incomprehensible language. Its meaning, however, was clear: *I'm scared, I'm scared.* . . .

"No, Paulie," he said at last. "No, no," he said, his voice

rising hysterically. "I thought you'd help me, but you want to kill me—"

"Georgie, I'm trying to help you!"

"I'll blow out," Georgie muttered as if talking to himself. "I got money. Three hundred bucks. That's money—" He broke off and moaned like a dog hit by a truck.

"You'll blow out and let the Spotter get away with it? Let him get away with what he's done to you and to Dutch?"

"I'm quitting the gang. What more d'you want? I'm quitting, Paulie. I'll get the money and blow."

"All right, go get it!"

"I can't go back alone, Paulie. I can't," he sobbed.

"Why can't you?"

"He'd be there."

"Who'll be there?"

"The Spotter!"

There was nothing left of the kid who once was game for anything; he'd been ground down. "Aw, snap out of it, Georgie," Paulie said softly. "The Spotter won't know 'til tomorrow that you didn't go through with Clip."

Georgie clutched the arm he couldn't see. "Paulie, he knows everything—"

"Okeh, Georgie," Paulie said in a soothing voice, as if sitting at the bedside of one of his sisters aroused by a nightmare.

"You've got to come with me, Paulie!"

"Sure, I'll come, Georgie."

He was thinking that maybe he could still change Georgie's mind about going to the station house, maybe he could convince Georgie to talk to Father McGinley. But if not, not. With the money, Georgie had a chance to break free....

Paulie pushed open the cellar door and led the way down the dimly lit hallway.

When Red McMann heard footsteps in the vestibule he slipped on his mask and, catlike, leaped up from his sitting position. He drew the gun from under his armpit.

"Stick 'em up!" he ordered Paulie. "This got nothin' to do wit' yuh!"

He had masked his face, but Georgie instantly recognized that hard, clipped voice. "Red!" he gasped. Blindly he tried to conceal himself behind Paulie, like a frightened child seeking the protection of a big brother.

Red McMann bolted to one side; the whiskey he'd drunk seemingly evaporated. "Outa my way, polack!" he yelled.

His arms tightening around Paulie, Georgie screamed. He'd forgotten that he, too, packed a gun. The redhead fired. Georgie dropped to the sidewalk, letting go his grip on Paulie, who plunged forward.

Paulie swung his fist at the masked gunman, felt the hard bone of a jaw against his knuckles and as he grappled with the man he had struck, the sidewalk seemed to lift like an elevator. They both fell.

Stunned, the gun slipped from Red McMann's fingers. Paulie seized him by the shoulders and slammed his head against the sidewalk. Dizzy, he half rose, then stooped to tear the mask from the unconscious gunman's face. He wouldn't have known it was Red McMann if Georgie hadn't called out the name of the bastard who so long ago had lured Dutch and himself up to the roof. Paulie's eyes swerved to Georgie crumpled on the sidewalk, not knowing whether he was dead or still alive, to the people who came from nowhere surrounding them in a noisy circle.

"Get an ambulance for Chrissake!" Paulie cried.

He wasn't thinking of what he had done. That he'd caught Red McMann with the goods. Caught him in the act. He wasn't thinking that he'd scored against the gang that had sucked in Dutch and Georgie like some filthy whirlpool. He wasn't thinking. Tears in his eyes, he was almost unaware of himself shouting at the onlookers: "That bastid shot Georgie! Tie'm up! Get a cop, somebody! Get an ambulance, somebody! Get Father McGinley over at Holy Cross! Get movin' for Chrissake! Get moving. . . ."

Paulie pillowed Georgie's head between his knees and gently stroked his forehead. Only now, like a little boy, did he begin to weep.

BENJAMIN APPEL grew up on the West Side of Manhattan, in the neighborhood known as Hell's Kitchen. With his first published novel *Brain Guy*—"a street corner *Macbeth*," Clifton Fadiman wrote in his review—he began to put down all he knew of its crime, poverty, and politics. Over the years his Hell's Kitchen fiction, which includes many of his short stories and six of his fifteen novels, has been highly praised by critics and writers alike and has become a permanent addition to contemporary American literature.